Dedalus European Classics
General Editor: Timothy Lane

Dark Vales

Raimon Casellas

Dark Vales

Translated from Catalan by Alan Yates
&
Edited by Eva Bosch

Dedalus

The translation of this work was supported by a grant from the Institut Ramon Llull.

Published in the UK by Dedalus Limited,
24-26, St Judith's Lane, Sawtry, Cambs, PE28 5XE
email: info@dedalusbooks.com
www.dedalusbooks.com

ISBN printed book 978 1 909232 61 7
ISBN ebook 978 1 909232 88 4

Dedalus is distributed in the USA by SCB Distributors,
15608 South New Century Drive, Gardena, CA 90248
email: info@scbdistributors.com   web: www.scbdistributors.com

Dedalus is distributed in Australia by Peribo Pty Ltd.
58, Beaumont Road, Mount Kuring-gai, N.S.W. 2080
email: info@peribo.com.au

Publishing History
First published in Catalan in 1901
First published by Dedalus in 2014

Dark Vales translation copyright © Alan Yates 2014

Printed in Finland by Bookwell
Typeset by Marie Lane

The Translator

Alan Yates, born in Northampton in 1944, is Emeritus Professor of Catalan at Sheffield University where he worked for 30 years, after graduation (1966) and then a doctorate (1971) from Cambridge. His teaching and research covered the language and the modern literature of the Catalan-speaking lands. He has published several books and numerous articles in these fields, now keeping a foot in both by exercising his enthusiasm for literary translation. The rest of his time (when not spent with grandchildren or being out and about on his local patch) is devoted to mountain walking and nostalgic fell-running.

The Editor

Eva Bosch is a painter, writer and video maker. She writes on prehistoric art, and has lectured on Picasso and Miró at the National Gallery, Tate Modern and the Instituto Cervantes. Born in Barcelona, she grew up in Figueró-Montmany, the village where *Dark Vales* takes place. In 1973, she fled the upheavals of Franco's regime to settle in the UK, where she studied at the Royal College of Art and later at the Rijksakademie van Beeldende Kunsten in Amsterdam. She now lives and works in London with regular sojourns in her home village, combining her creative work with lecturing in the History of Art.

Portrait of Raimon Casellas, c. 1898, by Ramon Casas Carbó.
(Charcoal on paper. © Museu Nacional d'Art de Catalunya, Barcelona.)

Contents

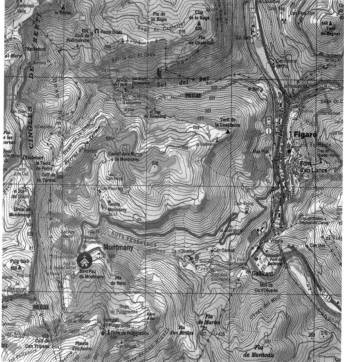

The Figueró-Montmany district of Catalonia.
(Fragment reproduced from the map "Cingles de Bertí",
courtesy of Editorial Alpina, Barcelona, 2013.)

Main street with donkey – Figueró around 1910.
(Courtesy of the Municipal Archive, Figueró-Montmany)

Introduction

The novelist and the novel in context

Raimon Casellas i Dou (b. Barcelona 1855) died, almost certainly by suicide, in 1910. The reasons for his premature death can be read between the lines of his novel *Els sots feréstecs*. The first edition appeared in Barcelona in 1901, although all of its chapters had previously been published between 1899 and 1900 in a Catalan newspaper. *Els sots feréstecs* is considered to be the first truly modern novel in Catalan.

Casellas was an extremely influential figure in Catalan *Modernisme*. This movement corresponded in broad terms to Art Nouveau and the European *fin de siècle*, and it left a major legacy on all artistic fronts. The architect Antoni Gaudí and contemporaries like Domènech i Muntaner and Puig i Cadafalch exemplified a revolution in style which also reverberated locally in every branch of the decorative arts. The young Picasso was formed in that setting, absorbing trends which were distinctive in outstanding Catalan painters like Ramon Casas, Santiago Rusiñol and Isidre Nonell. It is important to understand *Els sots feréstecs* as a manifestation of the same 'cultural revolution'.

Casellas was primarily an art historian and critic, but his novel *Els sots feréstecs*, and his two collections of short stories (*Les multituds*: 1906; *Llibre d'històries*: 1909) demonstrated a talent for giving literary form to his intellectual and artistic concerns.

Modernisme was superseded by the more sober cultural model of *Noucentisme* which prevailed in the first decades of the twentieth century. Casellas was torn between his own initial artistic idealism and the demands of a more disciplined programme. Class conflict and social turbulence, however, were exacerbated during the same period, and this undoubtedly contributed to the author's final disillusionment, perhaps anticipated already (intuitively and poetically) in his novel.

With input from *Modernisme* and then *Noucentisme*, the basis of twentieth-century Catalan politics and culture were established. These can be concisely defined as: organised demands for autonomy within the Spanish state, affirmation of cultural distinctiveness and consolidation of the status of the Catalan language. The Spanish Civil War (1936-1939) followed by the dictatorship of Francisco Franco led to a period of social and cultural repression with the suppression of the Catalan language and culture. After the death of Franco in 1975 things changed during Spain's difficult transition to democracy. The Spanish Constitution of 1978 gave the Catalan language special 'respect' and specific protection in the respective autonomy statutes of Catalonia (1979), Valencia (1982) and the Balearic Islands (1983). The new political context enable Catalan literature to recover its twentieth-century momentum and flourish again. A good illustration of this is the fact that the first edition of *Els sots feréstecs* with a scholarly introduction appeared in 1980, at a time when many other key writers from the pre-war period were being 'rediscovered'.

Els sots feréstecs/Dark Vales

Els sots feréstecs artistically converts an actual place into a 'landscape of the mind' (while the real location is endowed with a mythical aura derived from the fictional recreation).The novel is set in a rural region of Catalonia, centred on the parish of Montmany, some 40 kilometres north from Barcelona. The author's personal links with the area and with the parish priest there at the end of the nineteenth century are explained in the Editor's note. Nowadays Montmany is a

Introduction

more accessible place than it was in the late nineteenth century, but it retains much of its ruggedness, especially as most of the traditional subsistence agricultural activity has now disappeared. At the time when the novel was written this was a remote and forbidding 'back of beyond', the reason for the priest's exile, is the sin of heterodoxy. The ex-seminarian Casellas's feel for the territory is reflected in his novel to the extent that the words on the page can virtually be used as a guide for finding one's way around the whole district.

The author put a lot of himself into the novel and its central character. 'Intensity of feeling and of technique' had been highlighted by him as the main requirement for Catalan fiction in order to put the literature of his own country in line with the European *fin de siècle*. As a prominent historian and critic, Casellas was fully abreast of the currents which were transforming Western culture. One main agent in the intellectual ferment within which he was working was a preoccupation with the idea of a 'Godless universe' (derived from Schopenhauer and Nietzsche). Thus the Decadent morbidity which pervades *Dark Vales* is an effort to explore the bounds of human reason, which ran up against the inadequacy of language to communicate ultimate truths and the mysteries of the human condition. The frequent use of punctuation dots for pregnant pauses (a favourite Symbolist device) is intended to show moments of crisis where reason and words begin to fail and where silence itself is supremely expressive. In a similar way the constant reiteration throughout of key phrases and motifs is a literary application of Wagner's musical *Leitmotiven*. The notion of 'landscape of the mind' surfaces prominently here, and is complemented by Casellas's use of an earthy and rough-edged diction (at the time a notable innovation in literary Catalan) in presenting description, action and the characters' speech.

The translation aspires to be faithful to the principal stylistic features of the original: to render the subtle interplay between a landscape and the two minds which are central in *Dark Vales*: that of the narrator, merging with that of the main character. Casellas was writing at a time when the conventions of nineteenth-century realism, objectivity and the 'authority' of the omniscient, impersonal narrator, were being seriously questioned. Like many contemporary authors Casellas replaced the discredited omniscient narrator of conventional realism by inserting another consciousness in the narrative as a presence operating close to the level of a character's mind. This is particularly evident in the treatment of the priest-protagonist's dreams, visions and hallucinations, leading up to and then after his breakdown, from chapter XIV onwards. Especially innovative and challenging is the exploration of his 'locked in' catatonic condition in the final chapters, creating an 'atmosphere of the mind'. There are points in *Dark Vales* where the relationship between the two 'minds' comes close to breaking point and where fragmentation of traditional narrative structures and syntax seems imminent.

Characterisation is highly stylised. The figure of Father Llàtzer, has to bear a lot of weight, perhaps too much. This, however, is an inevitable consequence of how the story is told.The presentation of the atavistic rustics as an amorphous, subhuman mass reworks Zola's concept of *la bête humaine* in the light of contemporary trends in the new sciences of psychology, sociology and criminology. Monotony here is obviated by the presence of few minor characters: Aleix the truffle man, picked out of the anonymous peasant crowd in chapter I; pumpkin-faced Carbassot, feebler as a presence than Aleix, who figures in the interlude provided in chapter VI. This pairing is complemented by another one, the old couple who serve Father Llàtzer, and the local whore. The priest's household companions, Josep and Mariagna act as a double-act Sancho Panza to Father Llàtzer's Don Quixote. The inseparable pair supply an authentically human, and humane, dimension to a novel which, given the insistence of its symbolism and its prevailing bleakness of outlook, would be much the poorer and the more monotonous without them.

The striking and colourful figure of Footloose enlivens the action in her role as a caricature of the Decadent *femme fatale*: the embodiment of the forces of Evil, and ultimately of cosmic despair. Her name in Catalan, *La Roda-soques*, denotes both 'vagabond' and a woodland bird (treecreeper/nuthatch). It being impossible to

Introduction

convey in a single English word 'footloose (and fancy free)' was chosen.

The landscape of Montmany is the virtual protagonist in the novel, a feature enshrined in the Catalan title. For rendering *sots feréstecs* ('wild ravines/gorges') *Dark Vales* was chosen as it reflects the dominant emotional/psychological atmosphere of the narrative.

While it is difficult to dissociate the themes and the mood of *Dark Vales* from Raimon Casellas's suicide in 1910, the novel has a much wider and more complex relevance than that or than the work's religious trappings. Father Llàtzer can be seen as an archetype of the modern intellectual who aspires to improve, enlighten and dignify the society in which he lives. This grim parable about a parish priest who tries and fails to bring salvation to a benighted flock does not negate altogether a kind of nobility which inheres in the undertaking and in the efforts made to achieve it.

AY

Villagers from Can Mas and Ca l'Antic – around 1910.
(Courtesy of Mercè Pareras i Puig)

Editor's Note

The writings of Raimon Casellas were familiar to me from my childhood in the village of Figueró-Montmany in spite of Francoist censorship and the dictatorship's proscription of the Catalan language. Set at the very end of the nineteenth century, the events narrated in this highly original novel take place in the dark vales of the parish of Sant Pau, in the rugged foothills of the Pyrenees. With forbidding crags, thick woods and magical ponds, the bitter winters there deny it the prosperity, based on hot springs, of the neighbouring village. The dilapidated partly Romanesque church of Sant Pau still stands in the wild empty ravines, having borne witness since Casellas's day to poverty, revolts, and a bitter civil war. After the innumerable clumsy restorations it has suffered down the centuries, it is in danger now of succumbing finally to the fate so feared by Father Llàtzer.

In his youth, Raimon Casellas made several visits in those obscure yet enchanting valleys. He wrote later of going in 1870 to the Uià farm, fleeing from Barcelona with his mother during an outbreak of yellow fever in the city. With its 'cultivated terraces lining the hillside like steps rising up towards the clouds', the house there is a consistent point of geographical reference in the narrative. His intimate knowledge of the region is reflected in the geographical accuracy and emotional engagement of his descriptions.

The parish priest at the end of the nineteenth century was Father Lladó, who was on friendly terms with the young

Casellas (himself a seminary student). Local archives record Lladó's tussles to uphold in the district the authority of his own church. Conflicts between the clerical authorities and the villagers were to persist into my own childhood during the 1950s. It is likely that Lladó was the model for the central character in the book: the coincidence Lladó/Llàtzer is surely not accidental. The former was involved in ecclesiastical power struggles, whereas the fictional priest's personal drama contains a higher ambition: to break 'the umbilical cord that unites man to matter, thus freeing him from slavery', in the words of Jordi Castellanos. Làtzer, however, fatally underestimates the power of the flesh or the dark allure of the rocky slopes with natural forces haunting the deep ravines and the dim paths in the Black Wood.

The densely poetic language of the original poses a daunting task for the translator. For years I had harboured the dream of bringing this extraordinary work to a wider public. After persuading Alan that *Els sots feréstecs* was not 'untranslatable', the idea was transformed into an up-and-running project which acquired definitive momentum when Dedalus accepted the work for publication.

My specialism as a painter and a lecturer in art emphasises my own sensitivity to the geographical and atmospheric characteristics of the countryside where I grew up and where Casellas had chosen to set his novel. Co-operation in the translation process has enabled me moreover to revisit in a creative way the moods, local legends and traditions of the place. The whole operation has been a laborious one as we were constantly confronted with issues which stemmed from different, but complementary, perspectives on the text. My personal reading of it involves a painter's vision which inevitably suffuses my subjective responses to words on the page. I cannot but pursue a particular intimate suggestion emerging from a word or sentence, nor escape the idea that any translation can only be like a new layer painted on to a unique and precious fresco. Alan, on the other hand, had got involved in the project from within the disciplines of teaching and researching on modern Catalan language and literature, as well as having considerable experience of translating modern texts from that language into English. Our different backgrounds and cultural perspectives and our not completely coincident individual interpretations of the novel made for some intense, and ultimately productive, disputation.

Some general and two central problems concerning the translation are commented on in Alan's presentation above. 'Footloose' remains still a bone of contention between us. My own preference was for keeping the original Catalan nickname *La Roda-soques*, in the hope that the reader would overcome its foreignness. Alan, on the other hand insisted that it was necessary to seek some equivalence in English, along the lines he expounds above. Other thematic and stylistic issues presented by the challenging character of the original text were efficiently resolved by dint of exchanging and re-working numerous annotated drafts as the translation process evolved. The co-operation just described has given both of us much private and 'professional' fulfilment. The result, we think, is a worthy version of a unique and captivating novel.

EB

Religious Procession 1912
(Courtesy of the Municipal Archive, Figueró-Montmany)

Acknowledgements

Our thanks are due first of all to the Institut Ramon Llull for a grant from their programme of support for translation of Catalan literary works, and to Eric Lane and the Dedalus team for undertaking to publish *Dark Vales*. We are also grateful to Kim Eyre, for reading the English text and suggesting sensitive amendments; to Mike Mitchell and John Devlin for their encouragement, and for discussing various nuances of meaning and expression, pointing us towards improvements. The frontispiece map was kindly supplied by Josep Maria Mussachs of Editorial Alpina, Barcelona.

The builder, Josep Vilardebò i Puig, like Eva a native of Figueró-Montmany, was born in the Rovira house, a major landmark in the narrative. In the summer of 2011 he accompanied her and Jordi Castellanos on a tour of the whole district, sharing with them his memories and insights, pointing out hidden corners and identifying virtually all the buildings (most now in ruins) mentioned in the text.

Jordi, himself a son of the *sots feréstecs*, and the leading authority on the work of Raimon Casellas, tragically did not live to see this publication of *Dark Vales*, which would have given him such pride and satisfaction. The first English translation of the novel is dedicated to the memory of a special friend and generous mentor:

Jordi Castellanos i Vila
(Tagamanent, 11/9/1946 – Barcelona, 19/10/2012)

Cover of the first edition of *Els sots feréstecs*, 1901.
(Biblioteca de Catalunya)

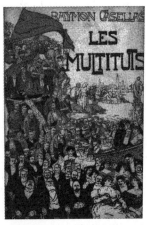

Cover of the first edition of *Les multituds*, 1906.
(Biblioteca de Catalunya)

I

Aleix the Truffle Man

Where, in the black name of the Devil, could the rotten bones of that old muckworm have gone to rest?

He was so damn doddering that folk believed he was over ninety, and there were those who would swear he was already well past a hundred. Some would even have wagered that his scraggy shoulders bore the weight of well over a hundred and fifteen or even a hundred and twenty years.

Among the shepherds of the rugged gorges of Montmany wild rumour had it that the old wretch had already been buried once, but because he had dark powers and was in league with the Devil and was very, very rich, he had struggled tooth and nail, they said, and managed to re-emerge from down below.

Once in a blue moon he would turn up at early Mass in the hilltop sanctuary of Puiggraciós, celebrated by a priest from another parish, and then everybody would look at him askance with a strange sort of malice where envy and perhaps even a certain admiration were combined.

'Who would give two cents for that old blighter...' would

say a puzzled cowman.

'And with that great stash of gold coins he must have, buried somewhere!' added a woodsman, with a knowing look.

'God blast him!' everybody else barked greedily. 'His coins ought to turn into scorpions!'

But what is certain is that none of those curses and sideways glances had any effect at all on him.

Hunched up with old age and with his head slumped, as if he was looking for needles on the ground, he shuffled clumsily by, pretending not to hear, confident in the two menacing great mastiffs with snarling fangs which, sniffing all around, went with him everywhere.

Whether for fear of the dogs or for fear of the old curmudgeon, children would run away in panic at the first sight of them. It was enough to shout, 'Watch out, here comes Aleix,' and all the youngsters would dash away to huddle in their mothers' skirts. Some of the older boys would approach him, if only to show off or to try to scrounge something from him:

'Aleix… give us a bit of loose change, will you?' one youth would say.

'Nah… nah,' was always the reply, grumbled darkly.

'Why not?'

''Cos I've not got no money, me.'

'Go on, you have so!'

'Nay, nah…'

'You do very nicely from your truffles…'

'Truffles… I don't go a-looking for them.'

To dodge further questions and scrounging from the boys, the old man would quickly turn tail. Those denizens of the near-deserted ravines of Montmany were left gawping and awkwardly wondering. Ever since their local parish priest went away they had been left to their own dumb devices, except for the occasional Sunday when they were summoned to Mass by the bell of Puiggraciós. Meanwhile, old Aleix, with an unbelievable agility for his age, would be heading steeply down towards the Uià valley, crossing the Rovira pine woods, along under the edge of the Bertí crags, into the dense trees of the shady lower slopes until he reached the Ensulsida col. Then like a snake sliding into its lying place he sidled into the half-ruined farmhouse of Romaní.

Those four cracked walls under a roof with more holes than tiles, like a star-embroidered sky, were his abode, his hiding place. At dawn every day, he used to set out from there heading towards the sun, to engage in the mysterious pursuit of his truffles.

'The damned things know how to bury themselves away right enough... but I can yank them out, sure I can,' he would mutter, twisting his frame and sniggering to himself.

And, by Jeebers, well might he laugh, because in the many long years he had been scouring all the nooks and crannies deep in those craggy, dark ravines he had got to know alright where the god-damned truffles were to be found, all snugly tucked away underground... Damn and blast them! To avoid being seen they choose the most hidden spots, the most isolated barren patches, the grimmest bits of ground... and because they are such shifty, slovenly layabouts they look for places which stay dampish even though well aired by breezes and warmed by the midday sun... That's why they seek shelter under trees with not too much cover, the hussies... to be able to lie around in the half-shade, with just enough sunlight and not too chilly...

From a hundred yards away the old man could tell the

chosen spots of the scented truffle; and whenever he went by a poplar, a holm oak or a walnut tree, he would cast a glance around the base of the trunk and would know instantly if there was anything there worth going for. The dogs went ahead of him, sniffing or yelping, as though trailing rabbits. The old man plodded on behind carrying a shoulder bag and a mattock in his hand. Hours and hours sometimes went by in this way... The dogs would be rooting about under brambles or under a poisonous sumac shrub, but as soon as he heard one of them bark, the old man would jump like a locust towards where the noise came from, and a glance was enough for him to size up the spot.

Whenever he saw that the earth was swollen in a sort of mound, he poked at it with the handle of his mattock. If the ground sounded even slightly hollow, old Aleix would smirk with satisfaction as if saying to himself, 'This is it!' To be certain that he had hit the right spot, the only thing needed was to see the swarm of purple flies that would have been attracted by the scent of the truffle... Then he would kneel down and carefully dig away, gently lifting layers of soil... until the coveted prize appeared. One by one he collected the truffles; one by one he lovingly cleaned them; one by one he caressed them with the palm of his hand... And, having contemplated them for a while – so lovely and black, so polished, so very fine and pretty – he put them deftly into his bag.

Then he made ready to go back to his lair... But before setting off, he would call his dogs, making sure that there was nobody to be seen round about... With his head close to the ground he listened for a while, and then from under the palms of both hands he scanned his surroundings... If it was all clear, he would head off at a shuffle towards his hiding place at Romaní. He had to be on the lookout, to keep a careful eye open, because those woodsmen of Ensulsida weren't to be trusted! Not to mention the nasty shepherds out on the low meadows! The Devil take them all!

That is why, when he arrived at the ruined farmstead, he could not resist sticking out his tongue to all those bloody rogues that envied his earnings. That is why he could never refrain from shaking an extended arm towards his neighbours' houses in the deep valleys below, with fist clenched, muttering his curse:

'Bugger the lot of you!'

It could be said that Aleix represented eternal temptation throughout the whole district of Montmany. The twisted figure of the old scarecrow, night and day filled the thoughts of the wretched folk living in the scattered houses of those steep-sided dark vales. Especially in the evenings, when men and women seated around a poorly burning fire were bolting mouthfuls of stale brown bread or taking deliberate swigs of rough wine. They could not drive out of their minds thoughts of the old man at Romaní, with so much money stashed away in the ground there. Murky plans of robbery or murder ran like blood-spattered phantoms through their torpid imaginations. Drowsily and mutely they were pondering the sinister idea that would not go away. Yet hardly ever was a word about it muttered. Then, when the trance was at its deepest, a shepherd would suddenly say 'I saw Aleix today'. And all would raise their heads, startled, as though waking up from a horrible obsessive nightmare upon suddenly hearing an echo of their own thoughts.

'And... where did you see him?' asked the farm owner, feigning indifference.

'T'were below Sunyer's terraces.'

'He must have been going into the village...' the farmer's wife insinuated.

'Or perhaps up to town...' said somebody else.

And once again there was a dreamy silence; they were all thinking about where he might have gone to, calculating the day of his return; imagining how much cash he would be bringing back from the sale of the truffles which fetched such a good price in town... After so many years spying on him, night and day, one could say that they were familiar with his every move. Adults and children knew that once every month he would take to the road, humping his load of truffles; that on his way back he would stop in Figueró to buy food and drink, and that he would always return carrying mutton joints and fresh bread in the folded corner of his blanket.

Not once but a hundred times, there had been someone who had thought of catching him unawares on the track and forcing him to hand over his money, or of firing off a shotgun at him, or of forcing him over the edge of the cliff... But these dark designs had never come to anything, because even the most unscrupulous plotters, when it came to taking real action, would feel a weird kind of fear when up against that mysterious man who, as the rumours went, had already been buried once and was in league with the Devil. And the terror inspired by the old man was the same as that felt by people about the ruined farm buildings at Romani. No one dared to go near there and, although the excuse was fear of the dogs, they were all in truth perturbed by the same thought: 'God knows what there might be behind the wuthering darkness of those half-collapsed walls!' When shepherds were within a stone's throw of the ruins, the very most they would dare to do was to make the dogs bark by slinging a rock at the building, before rushing away downhill, making the sign of the cross and muttering 'Jesus Christ!'

But then, one day, word went round that there had been no sight of Aleix anywhere in those parts. So many weeks had gone by and not a single soul had come across him, neither the shepherds with their flocks in the Brera woods nor the charcoal burners there working on the southern slopes. How or why he had disappeared was a complete mystery, but all of a sudden he was gone, as though the Devil had whisked him away. When the news began to spread through the ravines, passing quickly from one home to the next, a strange anxiety made the inhabitants' hearts race. There was talk of nothing else in each and every household:

'What might have happened?'

'Perhaps he's dead…'

'Maybe he's gone and left…'

'We ought to go up there to see.'

'There's nothing else for it!'

Even though none of them knew what the others were up to, members of all the scattered households were setting off towards the ruined farmstead, the men ruefully recalling the opportunities they had missed to settle their scores with the vile old fiend. One of them thought back to the day he had come across him high on the Bertí crags… and had not had the guts to push him over the edge. Another now regretted not having blasted off his shotgun at him that evening he caught sight of him down in the Rovira stream bed. 'How stupid of me!' they kept thinking to themselves. So strong were these persistent, upsetting thoughts that it was a struggle to hide them when they ran into other parties whose footsteps were guided by the same objective.

'Where are you going?' the question passed between them.

'We're heading for Romaní… What about you?'

'Same place.'

'We've been thinking maybe the old man is ill... and wondering if we can do anything for him.'

'That's just what we said: "perhaps there's something we can do to help..."'

The first group to reach Romaní, having taken every kind of precaution, found the farmstead empty. No sign of the old man, no dogs, no furniture, nothing to see anywhere. On the floor only garbage and rubble; cobwebs all over the walls; strands of ivy covering the cracks and holes. Their hearts were sinking fast, when they noticed that the earth just outside the threshold had been disturbed... Greed it was that spurred them all to rush towards that spot. They scrabbled in the ground and there they found a cavity, and inside the cavity an earthen pot. They looked at each other distrustfully, with sidelong glances, all of them wanting to get their hands on the treasure... But one hand was quicker than the rest to take off the lid, and they all saw that the pot contained no sign of anything. Some of the men raised a fist, as though vaguely threatening the accursed memory of the old curmudgeon who was having this kind of laugh at their expense.

'Six feet under is where he belongs!' some said.

'The Devil take him!' muttered the others.

Then, as they were going back down into their steep valleys, dejected and exhausted, cursing and swearing to themselves, to their ears there seemed to come a mocking voice from high up on the cliffs, saying:

'Bugger the lot of you!'

Some weeks, some months had gone by since then... until suddenly one day a shepherd from the Sunyers' farm thought that he saw Aleix among the topmost holm oaks in the Brera woods. 'Blast his eyes!' the shepherd exclaimed under his breath. 'Isn't that the old geezer? On my life it is and all! It's him alright!' That evening he told the assembled inhabitants of the farm all about it, as they were sitting by the fireside, everyone with a plateful of coarsely mashed potatoes in front of them:

'You wouldn't ever believe it... But today, up in the high thickets in Brera, I reckon I saw Aleix...'

'Are you sure?' asked old man Sunyer with an air of incredulity.

'I am that!' retorted the young lad.

'Never! No way!' chimed everybody else.

Such was their repeated insistence on this that the shepherd eventually thought to himself 'Maybe so, perhaps you did dream it...'

But the strange thing was that, a few days later, the swineherd from Malaric also thought that he had spotted the old man near the top of the Puiggraciós ridge. And the day after that, not just one or two but a whole lot of people had sighted him in several different places.

'Today I saw Aleix below Lledonell's terraces,' said Pau Boget to some shepherds who had met up above the Can Ripeta col.

'Me too: I saw him today in the oaks at Rovira,' replied one of their lads.

'And so did I, near the Black Wood,' said the shepherd from Can Prat.

'And what time was it when you saw him?'

'Me? It must have been at about a quarter to eight.'

'Same here; it wasn't yet eight o'clock.'

'Well... that's the same time that I came across him.'

And because everyone had seen him at the same time in

31

places so far away from each other, all those guardians of sheep and rams became very confused and worried, thinking about that devil of a man who had the marvellous gift of being able to appear at one extreme and another of the whole district, at precisely the very same time. And that anxiety among the shepherds soon spread again throughout the whole of Montmany. From then on, the bent and twisted figure of the old guy of Romaní became once again, night and day, their obsession: the ghost that haunted all those denizens of the tree-clad slopes.

'A devil of a man! Devil!' they would mutter deeply. 'It seems there's witchcraft afoot in all this.'

Some thought that a miracle could be the explanation; others believed that dark forces were at work.

'How can this ever be? To live longer than anybody else and to appear at the very same time in so many different places; for a man to melt away as if dead and then to turn up, just like that, slinking like a fox through valleys and over hills. How the flaming hell can this be, unless he has a pact with the wicked one?'

And some of them would make the sign of the cross with their thumbs, as though to repel the evil presence, mumbling as they did so:

'May God deliver us, may God protect us!'

And some others crossed themselves shakily, exclaiming:

'Jesus, Mary and Joseph!'

But, among all those strange and mysterious happenings, what perplexed them perhaps most of all was not being sure where Aleix sheltered after nightfall. Because everybody knew full well that he had not put his nose inside the tumbledown building at Romaní ever since the day he had seemed to melt away like a fine wisp of cloud.

For some days already the ruined walls of that hiding place had been taken over by the local shepherds and woodcutters. It became a storage site for tools and for the animals' nosebags, while sometimes they took the sheep inside to give them salt, so there was a constant coming and going of people in and out of the building.

So, if that was not where he spent the nights... where in God's name did the crafty old villain sleep? Certainly not in the open air, with the frosts and the downpours expected at that time of year. There was accommodation up at the sanctuary of Puiggraciós, but that was ruled out after someone had been to ask the couple who lived up there, and these wardens had said they had not seen him. The longer things continued like this, the deeper and shadier became the mystery of the old man's life.

Then it was that some of the locals said: 'Just a second! What if the old sod has booked in at the church for his nightly rests?' Their own parish church had been closed and completely abandoned for a long time, and now it served only as a roosting place for birds of prey which went in through the gaping windows. A strange idea, but perhaps true!

They went to have a good look around the outside of the building, they hammered time and again on the door and they peered through its small grill... to no avail. They saw the big birds flying to and fro along the cornice under the eaves, and they saw them perching on the altar stone in the apse, going in and out through the window. But of Aleix the truffle man... neither hide nor hair.

After all the times he had been regularly sighted, it was now quite the opposite and for days he had not been seen anywhere. 'Where can he have got to, where must he be, where has he ended up?' they all thought. Many had convinced themselves that he had simply melted away again, to reappear in due course... and then one Sunday suddenly he was sighted, high on the main ridge, heading towards Puiggraciós.

One after the other, the men playing cards in the stone yard outside the sanctuary gathered up the hands they had laid out, certain in their minds that now was the time to settle the score with Aleix. 'Now or never,' they were all thinking, 'It's now or never.'

'With all these comings and goings, one fine day he will take off for good with his pile of gold coins and we'll never again see hide nor hair of him.'

The same thought was in each and every mind:

'First, we get the youngsters to ask him for a hand-out... and then, as soon as his back is turned, one of us must try to jump on him, while the dogs are being clouted with sticks to fend them off.'

Aleix, meanwhile, was approaching the tables, sneering, as if he could sniff what was in their vindictive minds. The closer he came, the clearer it was to the card players that the old man had no dogs with him. And he looked really down and out, shabby and filthy... The children were just about to ask him for money, like they usually did... but then, as if he wanted to steal a march on them, old Aleix held out his own hand, just like a beggar, and in a pathetic, singsong voice started to plead:

'Good people... good people all... Won't you spare me a copper or two, for the love of God?'

Old and young were quite disarmed to hear that. Aleix, poverty stricken? Aleix without his dogs? Aleix without even a decent smock or shirt? Aleix asking them for money? In a trice all their greed was turned into raging anger, anger at being faced once again by a cruel reality.

'Go to Hell, to see if you can scrounge some blazing logs!'

shouted a woodcutter, bursting with rage.

Still sneering, the old man shuffled off without showing any sign of haste, thinking to himself that his clever bit of play acting had frightened away the scavengers for ever more.

'Nobody will bother me now… No more sleepless nights…' he kept muttering to himself.

And then, a short distance on his way, half hidden by some pine trees, he was unable to resist looking back towards the sanctuary and, with a devilish smirk, shaking his clenched fist he growled, gleefully now:

'Bugger the lot of you!'

Tree cutting in Vallcàrquera.
(Courtesy of Paquita Dosrius)

Peasant on horseback in Figueró.
(Courtesy of the Municipal Archive, Figueró-Montmany)

II

The Derelict Church

The Montmany folk had already been without their own priest for some months.

The last one to serve there had no alternative but to walk out on his parishioners. Old, sick and unable to fend for himself, he had been left suddenly on his own by the hard-nosed man and wife, both of them getting on in years, who had worked for him as sacristans and also as caretaker-gardeners. They were a grumpy couple who found fault with everything.

The wife, from dawn to dusk, used to talk endlessly about how she would prefer to die there and then, rather than to be stuck in that great ruin of a house with its scabby, flaking ceilings that were falling in on them. Every few minutes she would swear that she was weary and fed up of cleaning all day long that crumbling, dark church, with so many cracks that the damp got in everywhere, and so dank that the clothing on the holy images was falling to bits and the saints in their niches round the altars were all covered in mould. And her husband also used to moan, exclaiming that he was too old to do what he did… 'One minute it's water the vegetable patch and dig over the strip; then it's serve at Mass and ring the bells; next, go walking for hours at night escorting the holy sacraments up hill and down dale; then go and bring back this corpse or that one, and help dig the hole to bury them in…'

'We slog right enough for the plate of potatoes that we put into our mouths, sure we do!' the two used to be forever saying to one another, muttering out of earshot or just loudly enough for the poor priest to hear.

But things came to a head, and one day, full of confidence and guile, they went to see the priest to let him know that they were leaving him… Quite simple… they had been offered work looking after the shrine at Puiggraciós, because the couple doing that job were going off to live in the village… and it was an opportunity they couldn't afford to miss, because… and God himself could punish them for turning the chance down… Up there, on Sundays and feast days, there is some cash to be made from the people who go to drink in the canteen… And that sort of thing doesn't turn up every day out of the blue…

Listening sadly to this, the poor priest felt as though the whole cliffside had come crashing down on his head. Until that moment he had been fighting stoutly against the odds, bearing the heavy burden of ministering to the people in those deep, dark places where sadness reigned. But, on being told that his household companions were leaving him, he felt flattened and depressed, perplexed, as though weighed down all at once by all his previous woes. Seventy years was too long a time to have been going up and down mountain sides, trudging through mud and snow in order to say morning Mass at Puiggraciós and then, the same day, High Mass in the parish church, or to go and give the last rites or attend to the dying wishes of his scattered parishioners ensconced in the deep, wild recesses of that mountainous terrain.

More dead than alive, he was taken to Figueró, where he had some relatives, and from then onwards the house which had been his home was left deserted, abandoned, becoming just a heap of rubble shrouded in isolation.

The church building itself also had to be closed. But, before the door was finally locked and bolted, the nearest neighbours gathered at the entrance in order to see who was to look after the keys. In truth, nobody at all particularly wanted to take charge of them. Those denizens of the wooded valleys felt a certain fearful aversion towards anything to do with the temple and its altar... and the idea of being able to go freely in and out of the church, and of being in charge of all its contents, filled them with a kind of dread. From the oldest to the youngest, they all felt in awe of the vestments, of the sacramental ornaments, of the paten and the chalice. They knew that all these things were somehow the tableware and the clothing of God Almighty himself who has the power of life and death over all men, who brings thunder and lightning, who gives the sun its dazzling brightness and who makes it rise each day. There were those among them who would tremble in fright merely on coming close to those accessories of divine service. And so, even though they might have suffered the bleakest poverty and been starving to death, most of them would not have dared to lay a hand on the sacred vessels, for fear of being struck and laid underground by a bolt from Heaven while that sacrilege was being committed...

But there was more to it than that... for it was no secret to anyone that those poor treasures of the mountain temple were of very little value. It was widely known that the cruet dish was made of lead, that the chalice was copper and that all the vestments were nothing but darns from top to bottom. That is why, when the time came to close perhaps for ever the iron-studded doors of the church, and when someone asked: 'Who is taking the keys?' they all shrugged. Finally the people at Uià took charge of them, as this was the nearest house to the church.

From then on it seemed as though that landscape, with its ravines already drenched in shade and sadness, was finally engulfed in a limbo of gloom. The last peal of the bell marked the rapid fading into oblivion for the ceremonies of the blessed sacrament, the coming together of neighbours at every service of worship, the sermons delivered from the foot of the altar, the men singing up in the choristers' gallery, the pleasures felt when alms of festive cakes and small loaves were blessed... as though, in the blink of an eye, their last, tiny remnant of soul had flitted away from those surly parishioners of the dark vales.

If anybody wanted to attend Mass, on a holy day, they had to go to the one which was said at daybreak, up at Puiggraciós, by a priest from the nearby village of Ametlla. When a baby was born, it had to be taken for baptism to Saint Bartholomew's or to the church at Bertí. When a death occurred, any priest from thereabouts would go to the house and load the body on to the back of a mule, to carry it in this way to Montmany for burial in hallowed ground.

How very depressing was all this! Even the most slow-witted peasants felt deprived of something... something they just could not explain. And many of them said that it was a punishment, a spell that had been cast, a curse...

But the most painful and upsetting thing for them all was not to hear the bells ringing at any time of day. Everybody, however old or young, felt a strange anxiety, a kind of yearning for the voice which used to measure out for them the sad hours of their lives.

At eight o'clock in the morning, when Mass was announced by those three resounding chimes *ding... dong... ding...* followed by the final volley of repeated loud clangs, everybody who was out working at different places in the woods or on the cultivated terraces would take from their baskets the hunk of dark bread which was breakfast. At exactly midday, as soon as the twelve strokes sounded from the small belfry, everybody gathered up their tools, making ready to walk home if that was not too far from where they were working, or finding a patch of shade in which to sit and swallow what they had brought with them to bite upon. And then, especially in the evening, when the measured peal calling to prayer sounded out, it seemed as if even the oxen and the sheep recognised what it meant and they began to show signs of chafing to go homewards and into the yard...

Nobody but nobody could get used to the idea that the voice of the bells had been silenced for ever. When it rained, or when there was mist or low cloud, especially in winter, when the sun seems to hide itself in order not to show how time is passing, when all the land is clothed in gloom, the shepherds and the wood cutters out among the trees lost any instinctive sense of time... and they groped their way around a landscape that was blanketed in the mystery of darkness.

Weeks and then months went by in this way... and, because privation and misery can inure mankind to anything, there came the day when both shepherds and those who worked on the land became used to the bells' silence, to that particular silence which seemed to be that of death itself. They saw cracks gradually appearing in the church walls... but they paid

41

no particular heed. They saw a thick mat of nettles and mallow plants, sap-rich and proud, spreading like a crazy dishevelled lawn, overgrowing the narrow strip of the burial ground in the space between the priest's house and the church... but nobody took any notice. They saw ivy spreading everywhere, clinging like a bloodsucking parasite to the walls of the temple and to the stones enclosing the priest's vegetable garden, clinging even to the gnarled lower trunks of the cypresses in the cemetery, and nobody bothered about it. They had grown quite used to seeing how, in the early evening, big shadowy birds, wildly screeching, came and went through the windows of the church, as though that were their domain, their palace... The whole spectacle of desolation to which these people's lives had been condemned made no impression whatsoever upon them.

Only occasionally, when round by the church apse they glimpsed pairs of buzzards, circling as though in a witches' dance, in mysterious wheeling movements high in the air, only then did they feel a kind of shudder. Then they crossed themselves, murmuring a strange prayer that they knew by heart, in order to ward off evil. Otherwise, they were indifferent to everything. The slumbering spirit of these people of the wooded hills had become resigned to the dilapidation of the temple and to the silence of the belfry, just as they were resigned to a life of calamities and of grinding poverty.

Then one day a rumour started to go around, from one house to another, that a new priest was on his way, and the people were all mystified.

'A new priest!' they said. 'What must he have done wrong, for him to be sent here to do penance?'

III

The New Priest

And so, one afternoon, some local people out in the woods caught sight of a priest, he looked to be middle-aged, and was coming up from the direction of the Oliveres farmhouse, astride a mare and accompanied by an old man and his wife, who must have been his servants. The news travelled in whispers, from one ear to the next:

'He must have done something really wrong... and he's been brought up here to purge his sins.'

Far from being suspicious, the priest was completely ignorant of the mutterings that his arrival was causing. Still less could he guess that the malice of those woodlanders might be so refined when it came to sniffing out badness lying in the deep recesses of any secret.

He rode painfully on and on, up the arduous mountain route, eager to reach before dark the parish to which he had been appointed.

'The path is long and steep,' reflected the priest, filled with sad resignation. 'The path is long and steep... just like the rest of the journey that lies ahead before I find peace in my soul.'

But the deeper he penetrated into the dense solitude of the woods, the easier and the braver he came to feel. Suddenly, it seemed as if his spirits were being lifted by the view of the centuries-old trees, standing tall and serene before him, and by the invigorating fragrance of their resins that wafted gently over his drawn features. It was as though they were offering him a new life, putting out of sight his previous one, and erasing from his head the burning memory of his dreadful fall into disgrace, all those errors of judgement and all that excessive pride which had filled his heart, the causes of his exile.

The further he went into the shadowy mystery of the pinewoods, the more he felt his spirit easing. It was as if little by little, with every stretch of track covered, he was also leaving behind the heavy burden of his previous tribulations. He had not experienced such a sweet moment ever since the day of his repentance when, with tears pouring down his face, he had felt that the whole weight of his sorrow and remorse had been lifted from his chest. He was a natural dreamer, so all the contemplative urges embedded in his inner self were satiated now by the sight of the lofty crags and mysterious woods, to such an extent that he forgot the agony he had dragged along everywhere with him ever since that short time of wild delusion which had threatened to draw him into doctrinal revolt and to bring about his ruin.

'This is no exile; this will be my Paradise!' said the priest to himself, as he turned left from the valley and started up the rough climb to the Uià farm. 'What else could I ask for, Lord, as I approach old age, other than to be able to hide my afflictions in the peace of the mountains?'

Then, a thought came into his mind. Maybe the infinite

compassion of the Almighty, instead of punishing him for a moment of wrong-headed weakness, wanted rather to reward him for his repentance. From the depths of his heart he felt the swelling of an immense gratitude for the mercy of God who was guiding his steps towards the loneliness of those imposing surroundings.

'How beautiful is everything here, despite all its wildness!' exclaimed the priest, gazing at the mighty Bertí cliffs on his right, towering above him like an immense rampart built by gigantic arms at the beginning of Time. Admiration was springing abundantly forth deep inside him, bringing biblical words to his lips:

'Wondrous are your works, Lord, and no mouth is worthy enough to praise them.'

And, as though he could not contain the enthusiasm he felt, he was eager to infect his companions with it, asking them excitedly:

'Isn't all this admirable, Josep?'

'Yes, Father,' replied the old man, humbly respectful, while guiding the priest's mare by the halter.

'Don't you think this is beautiful, Mariagna?' said the priest, this time addressing the housekeeper who was coming along behind the mare, mounted on a mule carrying all their household goods packed in sacks, bundles and pillow cases.

And the poor old woman, nodding slightly, muttered respectfully:

'Yes, Father.'

Facing the dense forest in front of him, the new priest's eyes opened wide like those of a child, shining at the prospect of living and dying in peace, surrounded by the serenity of those wild, empty ravines. The only thing that slightly tightened his heart was coming across the occasional local who was going to or returning from Figueró village. He observed their surly demeanour, or the sideways looks they gave as they went by, seeming as they did to be asking how and why strangers were moving into the priest's house, as though resentful at the arrival of newcomers.

'Good afternoon to you!' the priest greeted them kindly.

'God be with ye,' replied the tongue-tied people on the track, with their heads bent and eyes cast down, as though embarrassed to return that greeting. But as soon as they had walked on for a few yards, they would turn their heads with a sly look, squinting to see what they could make of the outsiders, of how they looked or how they were dressed, or whether they were carrying much baggage…

'They are rough and craggy like the mountains they live in,' thought the priest, trying to make sense of the surly disposition of those people. 'The continuous struggle with a harsh land that can barely provide them with their daily bread also kills any love for their neighbour, and makes them mistrust everything… But I will win them round, if the Lord helps me… I will soften their hearts.' And, remembering the sacred text, he added:

'I shall sow seeds of sweetness amongst men.'

By now, the three of them had followed one another up to where the track levelled out and the black walls of the Uià farmstead were just coming into view. Being a man who knew his way around those parts, Josep went ahead of the other two to enter the property. Once he was in the yard, he heard the dogs barking as he shouted to those inside:

'Hallo, good people! God bless and keep you! I've been sent by Father Llàtzer, the new priest, to pick up the church keys.'

Meanwhile, the priest gently spurred on the mare to go

down again towards the house. But before beginning that descent... he took one last look back at the deep, narrow valley which, he thought, was to cut him off for ever from the world of the living. Then, as soon as he had a clear view forwards, his eyes were set anxiously on the drop that suddenly opened up before him... Deep down in the middle of the ravine he sighted the stunted little belfry of the church, and then the badly weathered walls of the house that was to be his home. The moment he identified them, he felt a kind of panic. Everything about that lonely corner looked ruinous, lost and engulfed in murky sadness among the cypress trees and the overgrown grass of the graveyard.

'Is this where you are sending me to live, my Lord God?' thought the priest, his heart gripped with anguish. Meanwhile, from the high windows of Uià, the heads of the people there peered out as if to welcome him and his companions. The owner, a blind old man who was a bit simple minded, limply waved a shaky hand, in a vague greeting. His wife, a woman with protruding jaws, younger than the blind man, merely stared inquisitively at the visitors, as if trying to take them in all at once with her eyes.

The mien of those outlandish folk who were to be among his closest neighbours, combined with the view of the shadowy ravine, the deep hole of sadness that he was about to enter as though to be buried alive there, everything filled the priest with desolation. His white-haired head dropped forward on to his chest as a feeling of great dismay weighed down upon him.

Then, making an effort to recover, he said to his aged companions:

'Right, let us be off!' speaking as though eager to get through once and for all the last stage of the Calvary that, at first, he had taken for Paradise.

View of L'Ullà 1950
(Courtesy of the Municipal Archive, Figueró-Montmany)

La Rovira
(Courtesy of Josep Vilardebò i Puig)

IV

Death's Dominion

Josep went in front, as a guide; then came the priest astride the mare; behind him, Mariagna and the bundle with their possessions on the back of the mule. And, somewhat ruefully, they made their way ever further into the shadow-filled ravine where, from that time on, they would be living as exiles from the world of men.

Then it was that a deep, deep sorrow came upon Father Llàtzer when he saw how, as he drew nearer to their destination, the circle of crags all around seemed to be closing in upon him, cutting off any retreat, as though he were being walled up on every side, until he would finally be buried in those depths! In front of him there reared up the dark northern bluffs of Rovira, crowned by the heights of Puiggraciós. To his right he could see, like a continuous wall reaching skywards, the ghostly rock shapes of the Bertí cliffs. On his left he had the cultivated terraces of Uià, lining the hillside like steps rising up towards the clouds. And at his back, merging gradually into those terraces, there stood out the great shoulder of Romaní, with the Castell dels Moros, the Moors' Castle, prominently outlined on the very top, like the head of a ghost. Rocks, hillocks, terraces, sheer cliffs, ridges, all joined hands on every side, forming a ring of black mountains that were terrifying to behold.

Entombed down there, the priest felt chilled to the bone, struck by a vague fear that the rocky pinnacles on every side were about to topple on to him. Completely shut in, he kept glancing around instinctively, as though looking for a way out, or at least to be able to see further. But it was in vain, totally in vain... There were no gaps or openings through which his eyes might range freely... Everything was enclosed, completely blocked off, walled in... Distance was eliminated by the lowering crags that imprisoned him... The word horizon had no meaning there... and he had to bend his neck backwards in order to see any sky above the encirclement of bulky hillsides and high tops.

The sun was still hovering on the point of dropping down behind the ridge... and great patches of shadow were spreading everywhere. The mystery of twilight was steadily taking possession of those rock clefts, wooded slopes and steep cliffs. Such awful dread struck into Father Llàtzer as he watched darkness advancing rapidly to settle upon the eternal solitude and silence of those hollows, which seemed to be night's permanent domain!

There were three or four isolated houses not far away, but their existence only made that sunken, barren place seem even wilder and lonelier. Beyond Uià, the moss-clad walls of the Rovira farmhouse could just vaguely be made out, almost completely concealed in the darkness of a thick clump of holm oaks; further away the smaller dwellings of Can Pere Mestre and Can Pugna were scarcely visible, huddled at the base of the cliff, as though terror-stricken; in the far distance, beneath the Castell dels Moros, it was nigh impossible to detect the shape of the ruined homestead of Romaní, with its remaining walls battered by hard times and by age, bent askew as though slumping with drowsiness.

Except for those dwellings, tucked into the contours of the land like animals' lairs, there was no sign of human habitation other than the priest's house and the church, in the middle of the dismal valley, linked together by the dark, dark green patch which was the cemetery. To come across any other houses scattered thereabouts, one had to climb sharply and nimbly up to the Puiggraciós ridge, or to scramble even more steeply upwards over broken ground to the Can Ripeta col, or to cross over the encircling jagged spurs and then drop through rough terrain into the neighbouring ravines, clattering steeply down to Can Sunyer or through the shady Black Wood to Can Prat below its hillside where the sun never lingered...

When the priest and his companions reached their new home, the sun had already gone right down behind the cliffs. Darkness was rapidly taking over the ring of rugged mountains. It was as though the air was being filled with black flecks that drifted down from the sky, forming quivering shadows everywhere in the valley.

'Open the door, Josep!' ordered the priest, while he and the old housekeeper were dismounting on the stone flags outside the doorway.

From the bunch of keys he was holding, the old man found the one which fitted the lock, fumbling to turn it, then opening the door with a push... and all three of them froze in horror when, having taken one step inside, they became aware of the rubble that lay everywhere. Dislodged blocks of stone, slabs of plaster on the floor, beam ends hanging down, this was the grim state of the house entrance, which seemed to be lamenting all the tragic destitution of buildings left to crumble. The old man and his wife wanted to take the bundle and the animals inside, to get everything under cover and unloaded wherever they could; but everywhere they stumbled over piles of debris. They first had to push heaps of rubble and stones away into corners, in order to be able to move about at all on the floor.

Such dereliction! Such utter desolation! The poor priest could not have felt more dispirited. With his arms drooping, all he could do was to shake his head slowly as he contemplated that half-ruined hideout which from then on was to be his dwelling. As he reflected that what was happening to him was a kind of burial of the last days of his old age – before he went forever more to the real grave of death itself – he was overcome by a feeling of utter helplessness that made him shudder with dread and anguish.

'No... the hour of eternal peace has not yet come,' he muttered as though from within a deeply disturbing dream. 'No... I thought that hour was so close, so close at hand... but now it is going further and further away... because I am still not fully cleansed of earthly concerns...'

But then, all at once, with a start, he drew himself up, as though goaded by an idea that suddenly brought him out of his trance. 'What about the church?' he thought. 'What kind of state must the poor church be in? Will it be just as tumble-down as this?'

'Josep!'

'Yes, Father...'

'Leave all this for now... and let us go over to the church... I want to see the church before night closes in...'

On hearing this from the priest, the old couple gave up their noisy efforts to clear the floor of the house, and all three of them now went outside, one after the other, heading together towards the graveyard. But once more they ran into the mysterious obstacles that were everywhere under their feet. The thick, dense tangle of grass covering the whole of the cemetery, overgrowing even the tallest of the funerary crosses, prevented them from reaching the walls of the church. It was as though everything they encountered – vegetation, people or stones – bore them a grudge, as though everything was conspiring to stand against them as outsiders who had come to disturb the silence of dead things and of places in deep slumber...

Father Llàtzer even thought that he could hear pathetic voices, seeming to come from below the ground, painfully complaining: 'Don't make a noise, for pity's sake! Don't make such a din! We were sleeping so peacefully... so gently... Why have you come to torment us now, when we had fallen so soundly asleep? And such soft slumber! Don't disturb people who are sleeping, nor the dead who lie at rest nor the ruins that are dreaming... We do not say anything at all to you... So do not make a disturbance... Don't wake us from our slumber...'

But Josep must not have heard these voices and their pained lamentations, as he was doing his utmost to overcome the treacherous vegetation covering the graveyard. Heaving hard, the old man was wrestling to force a way through the tangled growth, or stamping it down with his feet. Thus the priest was able to come along behind him through luxuriant mallow plants that were nourished by the slime oozing from corpses.

Having gone through the graveyard, they reached the door of the church and immediately tried to unlock it. But they were sorely upset when once again their efforts were thwarted... It was as though centuries of rust had built up inside the lock.

The priest, the old man and his wife, all of them strained to free it. But, despite all their efforts, the big bolt could not or would not be moved. And the lock made an angry grating sound, as though saying, 'So now you want to discover what secrets are sleeping inside here? Now you villains have come to rouse the mysterious spirit of the church, have you? Well, you shall not open the door; you shall not come in...' But the intruders applied such force that the door, creaking and groaning, finally gave way, at the same time as a terrifying uproar arose inside the nave of the church. It was the great big birds that had been roosting here and there in the building, now creating such a squawking racket upon being disturbed, such a screeching and a wild flapping of wings, as they flew out through the windows, like a throng of evil spirits.

Terrified by that demonic uproar which caused them great confusion, the three of them, all equally disconcerted, looked anxiously into the nave, without being able to make anything out. It was all in complete darkness, pitch-black darkness. The shadows had thickened so quickly inside there that the altar, the side chapels, the statues of saints and the presbytery were all enveloped in gloom. The faint starlight that could still be made out up by the windows had the effect of concentrating the darkness of their surroundings at ground level. Like souls in torment, the priest and the old couple, groping their way around in that blackness, finally found a piece of taper resting on a candle holder near to the font. The old man lit it and, now holding the tiny flame, was making his way carefully forwards, towards the presbytery, when he noticed that the floor was awash. Over time the rain, dripping in through the cracks in the vaulted roof, had formed a single expanse of shallow water over the uneven slabs beneath his feet...

'Lord! Lord!' exclaimed Father Llàtzer with his head in his

hands. 'Lord, do not abandon me like this! Do not punish me in this way, for I am still too weak to bear such tribulation!'

Josep, meanwhile, had reached the high altar and was lighting the candle stubs that he found on the side table... And in the flickering glow they all gazed in horror at the eerie sight of the saints and the statues behind the altar itself. The dust, the damp and the grime covering everything endowed those images and trophies with the faded, repulsive look of things that had been lying buried in the ground... The twisted columns, adorned with sculpted bunches of grapes and with angel heads, all formerly covered with gold leaf, were now clothed in thick mould, as though they were afflicted with a gruesome disease. The stocky figure of Saint Paul, patron saint of the parish, occupying his rightful place in the central niche, was hardly recognisable because it was riddled with woodworm and draped in cobwebs. One of Saint Isidore's arms was hanging loose... Saint Sebastian was leaning to one side as though about to topple over...

The priest was beginning to think that, just like the inhabitants of those dark vales, all the saints by the altar were also slumbering in the soporous shadows of the ruins. Could the pitiable images really be asleep? Or perhaps not, perhaps they were not sleeping... Perhaps it was worse than that... Perhaps they were dead, yes... dead and already buried. Because... thinking about it, their clothing, their tunics and mantles, looked like nothing other than shrouds, shrouds that had rotted in the ground and were now falling apart, revealing the wooden carcasses inside...

The priest was unable to bear that terrible vision any longer. He felt dizzy, a lump came to his throat and his legs were about to give way... He could stand it no longer, no longer... and he staggered outside. He would have called for help... But where would help have come from? The nearest neighbours were far away… and perhaps they were dead as well! He would have tried to flee… but where to? All the tracks and ways were obliterated by the blackness of night… Had he forgotten that he was a prisoner of the cliff faces and the hills around?

'Lord, have mercy!' he shouted, raising his arms aloft. 'Lord, have mercy!'

And, seeing in front of him the ruined house and the weed-infested graveyard… then the ring of black mountains walling him in on every side… he sobbed and broke down in tears…

V

Nightmare

'Josep!'

'Yes, Father…'

'Mariagna!'

'Father…'

'Look… I have decided to call the people of the parish to a meeting, here at my house. I need to find out if, despite the coldness in the very core of their being, I can make them blush with shame by showing them the sorry state the church is in. I want to see if God can touch the hearts of the walking dead here in these dismal dark vales, and if He can bring them back to life again… So then, Josep, you will go up to Puiggraciós and tell all the people who live around there; then you will drop down to the next valleys, and tell everybody to come along on Sunday, at mid-morning… Say that I have to speak to them… that I must see them… Is that clear, Josep?'

'Yes, Father.'

'And you, Mariagna, will go and invite the parishioners from all the houses close by here.'

'Very well, Father.'

'On Sunday, everybody here!'

That morning Father Llàtzer was feeling better, more positive. He had been battered by his long journey of the day before and by the shocks inflicted on his spirit by the vision of that savage world in ruins where it was his lot to live from now on. In spite of all this, he had awoken that morning in a quite calm and decisive state of mind, feeling infused now and then with that faith which can perform miracles and can move mountains... And yet... he had spent such a dreadful night, long feverish hours of nightmares and morbid visions. Such delirium! Such sinister aberrations!

He had dreamed that he was being buried alive inside a huge, deep hole in the ground, its sides walled with black mountains. He was shouting as loud as he could, his hair standing on end: 'Look what you are doing to me, burying me while I'm still alive and breathing!' 'It matters not at all,' came voices from the depths of the abyss. 'It matters not... It's the same for everybody down here, we're buried; all of us here are half corpse, half living thing...' And so indeed it was, because he had only to look all around his dreamscape to see that the great pit he was in was one immense cemetery, with only darkness and solitude. The houses he could see here and there were nothing but graves and family vaults... and the dejected people who dwelt in them, nothing but lifeless bodies. Through all the hours of night, when silence falls and everywhere is blackness, this spectacle of deadness takes over completely. As soon as the sun has gone down, men, women and children bury themselves in their own houses and, with their bedclothes as shrouds, they lie for hour after hour on the burial mounds which they think are their beds. When day breaks, because brightness comes to their eyes and birdsong to their ears, they think they are returning to life... But all that is fake and deceit... Death continues to reign, still... and as the first rays of light hesitantly appear, the dead leave their houses, some with a hoe on their shoulder, some with a shepherd's bag on their back. Like spirits from another world, all of them march unhesitatingly in the shade of the woods, as though sure of where they are heading and of which way to go. They eat, they drink, they walk, they stop, they till the earth, they lead their flocks to graze... And all their actions are performed blindly, without any conscious purpose. They do things just because they have seen these things done by other dead beings, their parents or grandparents, in times gone by. The dead do not think, and only from instinct do they follow the half-effaced tracks bequeathed to them from centuries ago... Nor are they touched by anything like love, except love for that quietude in which they are perpetually enveloped... Not to be disturbed is all they want. Not to be troubled or upset... To be left alone...

'What a vision of damnation! Lord, what damnation!' murmured the priest as he struggled with all the anguish of his dream. 'But I, what have I got to do with those dumb ghosts? I am alive, I can think, I have the will to struggle, I can love... So why am I being buried alive here?' 'They are burying you here as a punishment,' came the reply from the depths of the abyss. 'You, in your vanity and presumption, tried to dazzle people with marvellous clever ideas. You wanted to resurrect an ancient philosopher, a wise man from centuries ago, who had been completely forgotten by everybody. It was your vanity that made you pry into the sealed tomb that his writings had become, disturbing the mould on his books, their pages riddled with wormholes and sinful ideas. Out of vanity you claimed that universal truth was to be found there. And as your arrogance became ever stronger, you attempted to turn that heretic into a saint… That is why you have been exiled to this land of the dead, inundated with darkness and sorrow. That is why you must now live rubbing shoulders with the deceased who wander these black woods looking and behaving as though they were living beings possessed of souls.

That awful dream of his first night in Montmany stayed imprinted in the poor priest's mind like an image of woe and keening. He felt a strong need to tear it out of his head, in order to be able to embark with vigour on the redemption of the deprived shepherds and peasants of his parish. However, quite unaccountably, his memory was promptly filled again with the procession of dark figures which drifted sleepily back and forth in that limbo, unable ever to open their eyes to the radiance of life.

Thus, when the next Sunday word came to him that his parishioners had turned up and were waiting for him in the cemetery, Father Llàtzer was seized by a strange anxiety at the mere thought of coming face to face with them. For they were the same ill-fated woodland dwellers whom he had seen in his dream wandering like ghosts through the slumbering landscape, silently entering and leaving the tombs in which they dwelled.

As well as by these thoughts, he was tormented by something else: how to address those people in order to make himself understood… He had given classes in lecture rooms, and he knew what sort of language was right for communicating with his pupils; he had preached a thousand times in city churches, and he knew how to work the feelings of an educated congregation; he had disputed with some of the finest minds of his day, and he had the gift of swaying learned men by dint of argument. But… he had never before confronted such a lifeless audience as this one, and he did not know how to speak to them. He was overcome with doubts and anxiousness, and his stride seemed to falter...

'Father, they are all waiting...' said Josep.

'Yes, yes... I'm coming.'

And stepping out of his house, he said to himself, as though asking for inspiration from Heaven: 'How am I to persuade them? What can I say to stir them? Which might be the best words to raise the dead?'

Funeral at Can Plans, 1920s.
(Courtesy of Josep Tordera)

VI

Dwellers in Limbo

Moving along as smartly as they could, doddery greybeards and heads of households, all the menfolk of the parish had made their way to the hollow where the church stood, to see what the new priest wanted.

Those who descended there from the houses high on the Ocata ridge, did not look as joyless as the ones who had climbed up from way down below: the clothes they wore were not as dark, nor did they look so surly. Some of them, having arrived around the same time at the Can Ripeta col, had even walked together all the way down to the church buildings. And now an occasional remark passed between the older men, as when the one from Can Janet would say the odd word to his counterpart from Malaric or from Polonell or to gaffer Carbassot.

But the men who arrived from down in the ravines, either over the rocky slopes of Sunyer or by the dim paths in the Black Wood, could not have displayed a more dull-brained attitude nor more haggard looks. Such were their bearing and their appearance, so drowsily did they move their eyes, so unattractive was their whole aspect, so cowering their mien, that they looked more than anything like a line of praying mantises in a stubble field. Almost all of them wore suits that were too big for them, of a rough napped fabric, originally very dark in colour but now faded through the abrasion of brushwood or of clods of earth, a cloth which, if it had at first been black before turning a sort of dirty ash colour, had finally taken on an indeterminate, drab and muddy hue, 'the colour of a dog running away' as they themselves would have said... The whole company formed a turbid stain in that space, a blot of earth and dust, seemingly made by a gathering of people who, having lain buried for a long time, had risen from below ground in order to be present at the appointment.

It was a feeble-minded and taciturn assembly. They barely exchanged greetings, as though it pained them to utter a single word. While some sat on the stone ledges at the edge of the cemetery, others huddled against the church wall or with their backs to the crumbling stones of the priest's house.

There were no absentees at all among the parishioners who lived closest by. Almost all of them were decrepit, with sores and other visible signs of infirmity, like worn out hacks ready for the knacker's yard. Here was old man Pugna, encumbered with a goitre so big that it went right from the back of his neck to under his chin. There was Pere Mestre, with one leg shorter than the other and the painful limp that made him grimace. Then came the old devil who stayed up at Romaní, Aleix the truffle man, writhing like a snake and smirking. Over there, standing slightly apart, as though resentful about sharing the company of so many aged and infirm, one could see Cosme from the Rovira farmstead, with his blotchy face, tall and slender like a poplar tree. The blind man from Uià was sitting by the door of the priest's house, next to daft Joe, Bepus, the farm tenant, who would not let the old man out of his sight, unless the wife was keeping an eye on him...

Although so many people were gathered together, there was everywhere in the air a strange kind of stillness, as though all those men had the mysterious gift of being able to move about silently, without uttering a word, without breathing or causing even the slightest rustle. One was there with his head in the palm of his hand, as though asleep; another, as if in a trance, just stared at the heaps of freshly cut grass in the cemetery; there was one, with an ash stave held tightly in his fingers, who gently scraped the ground in front of him; and another who stood open-mouthed and with eyes closed, like an idiot.

When Father Llàtzer appeared at his doorway, they turned momentarily to look in his direction as though to size up the new priest, only to sink back immediately into their habitual torpor. The thick-skinned backwoodsmen were not impressed by the good looks of the priest or the kindly expression on his face, nor by the pained emotion that quivered on his lips, nor by the gleam in his still youthful eyes, seemingly at odds with his head of snowy-white hair. If anything, they looked embarrassed and intimidated in the presence of that embodiment of aching benevolence.

The priest gazed at them long and hard... and he could do nothing to prevent his mind from being filled once again with images of death. There before his eyes, that gathering of parishioners sitting around on the level ground of the cemetery, so burdened and depressed, seemed to him to be the representation of all the dispirited humanity that for centuries had lived out their lives in those grim environs. Under the earth, in the peace and tranquillity of death, lay the preceding generations. Upon the surface of the graveyard the present-day generations were here and there, almost as ashen and somnolent as those below who were lying in eternal slumber… But the priest was horrified by that idea, and so he rubbed his brow, as though to wipe away the haunting vision that once more intruded upon his thoughts. What he needed at that moment were not dark visions or depressing images, if he was going to touch the hearts of the sluggish rustics. Faith was what he needed, a burning faith in the resurrection of the dead… He needed charity, all-redeeming charity, in order to liberate those benighted souls who were wandering aimlessly in the darkness of limbo…

And then, as though struggling to bring to his lips the words of compassion which in previous times had come so readily to him, he addressed his parishioners, spreading his arms in the gesture of a father about to speak to his family, full of tenderness.

'My sons, I have called you here because… as you can well see… the poor church is going to rack and ruin… and we must see if we can repair it by all of us working together. Take a look inside there, for pity's sake… and tell me if you are not deeply saddened by such neglect. The first time I entered there, I could not hold back my tears… I know, I know that in these ravines where you live, in these vales of tears no less, poverty and desolation rule. But think on it: my own house is in ruins, and I have had to make my home in the entrance porch, which is holding up but only just… And I imagine that what I have to put up with will be the same for all of you. But, no matter what hardship we have to bear, a corner in which to take shelter, to find protection at night from the wind and the rain, we all have this much, all of us… except God! The church looks like a homestead that the children of the family have abandoned. Everything is collapsing, there are cracks everywhere, the roof is falling in, the walls are crumbling, and birds of prey are nesting on the cornices and roosting inside the apse... And are you not distressed by this, my children? Do you never hear remorseful voices calling to you: "You have a home... while God has nowhere. God has no roof over his head... and rain pours into the church..."?'

Most of his parishioners listened gawkily to this harangue from the priest, without showing any reaction. The less doltish-looking among them went no further than to move their heads indecisively, without giving away whether they were in agreement or not. In spite of this, the priest seemed not to lose heart, as though he felt that by dint of showing kindness and indulgence he would have the strength to win them over and to inspire them with the same fervour that was seething in his heart.

'What is more, my dear children, you must think of this... that God's temple is also the holy patrimony of his faithful followers, the hearth and home of Christian families. Never forget that within these walls which are now falling down other generations have come to pray and to find sanctuary: your parents, your grandparents, all your ancestors. Do not forget that in the nave there your own heads were sprinkled with baptismal water, when you came into the world; that there as children you were taught the holy commandments. Remember that there you were bound for life to the woman you have loved. Remember too how you came there to say the last prayer for your departed loved ones, before laying them in the ground... This house of God which has rejoiced in your gladness and lamented with you in your sorrows, how can you now leave it alone and desolate, locked... falling into ruins? Do you really want to commit to eternal silence these bells which have chimed merrily at your christenings and which have mourned the deaths of your nearest and dearest? Do you not miss the friendly voice greeting you in the morning and bidding you good night, awakening you and seeing you off to sleep, announcing storms or fair weather, calling you to festivities or to prayer and counting out for you the hours of the day? Do you not miss the sound of the bells? Tell me! Do you not miss it?'

The peasants said not a word. Even when assailed point-blank by the priest's blazing questions, they could make no reply nor show any reaction at all. They just looked pained and worried, as though bewildered by the new incumbent's exaltation as he did his utmost to wrest them from their eternal torpor. It was apparent that they felt ill at ease, painfully uncomfortable… that they were being goaded and made to feel a strange distress… They did not know what to do or how to behave. Some of them clicked their tongues; others tapped the ground with their feet… One man wriggled a finger in his ear, another scratched his head…

'How like creatures of the woods they are!' thought the priest, filled with anxiety, as he confronted that silence. 'Like moles underground, slinking in the winding depths of the mountains where they burrow… They hate to be disturbed, as though turning their backs on life. They would rather sleep submissively in the gloom than make their way towards the light. So much time spent in the dark has destroyed their sight, just as they have lost the power of speech from living in isolation…' The poor priest felt a shiver of unease and foreboding, sensing uncertainty about his ability to open their eyes and to make them open their mouths. And what aggravated this depressing feeling was that, in beginning to lose his hope of resuscitating them, there was being roused inside him a different emotion which he was horrified to acknowledge. In the place of brotherly love and commiseration, he was beginning to feel hostility, resentful hostility and loathing for those sullen people whose eyes did not leave the ground and who could not utter a word.

'But please say something, for pity's sake!' Father Llàtzer shouted. 'Speak just one word! You seem to be dumb... or dead... Oh, my Lord God! Dead!'

With this they began to recite all their miseries, the eternal litany of complaints they would voice whenever their affairs were pried into.

'We are so poor...'

'We are short of so many things...'

'We are so behind with our rent...'

'The last harvest was so lean...

'So many of our animals have died...'

'Things are so very hard...'

'But I am asking you not for material possessions or for money, good God above!' the priest said, starting to feel impatient. 'I am asking you only for hearts, spirits, arms that might help me, bodies that can move, legs that can walk... All I am asking for is willpower, just a little strength of will! The building work needed on our poor church can be done by our own labours. I'll get one or two skilled craftsmen to come up from Ametlla village, but you must help me in the holy work of restoring God's temple... Those of you who have pine trees on your land can bring trunks to form scaffolding; those living near the cliffs can lay stone surfaces on the tracks leading to here; along the way up from Uià there is enough limestone to produce several loads from a kiln, for cement; we can bring up from the stream below the mill as much sand as might be needed...'

They all stayed silent, as though not understanding what they were hearing.

'You mean that you refuse to do anything for the church!' exclaimed the priest indignantly. 'You refuse to do anything for God!'

Not a word was heard. Everyone stayed silent. The priest was looking at them, his eyes full of rage... and again there came into his mind the manic idea that the whole throng which he saw before him was nothing but a flock of animals. 'Beasts of the field... Wild creatures that inhabit the woods... They even have that look about them, and the same way of behaving! God forgive me if I am in sin!' he thought, 'but I cannot rid myself of this infernal fixation. That is what they are. That's what they are! It is enough to look at that man with the double chin and watery eyes to see that he is an ox, every bit an ox. And that one, with his round face and startled eyes, and his little pointy nose... that's it, he's an owl. Then him over there, with his sagging goitre and lumps all over his head, looks like a toad... And that other one, with the bad limp, he's a frog, when he does his strange sort of hops. God forgive me! God forgive me!' And horrified by his own thoughts which seemed like surges of madness, the priest stood forth, raising a compassionate arm, and said to his rustic parishioners:

'Go away, leave in the name of God. And may the Lord bless you all!'

The woodlanders were waiting to hear nothing else. They all turned tail and left, one of them slipping away towards the Ocata ridge, another disappearing in the direction of the Black Wood, each of them seeking their lair, in order once more to bury themselves alive.

Those who were going the same way muttered quietly:

'What a palaver the priest man came out with!'

'Gobbledygook!'

'And that crazed look in his eye…'

'There's something not right about him!'

Others smiled with an air of mockery:

'Go on then… build his new church for him,' said Pere Mestre as he limped along.

'That's it…' replied old man Pugna, making his goitre wobble. 'And meanwhile my house is falling to pieces…'

'Mine's damn-near collapsed already…' added the Truffle Man, smirking.

El Bellver, Figueró-Montmany
(Courtesy of Paquita Dosrius)

View of L'Ullà, 1960s.
(Courtesy of the Municipal Archive, Figueró-Montmany)

VII

The Local Entertainer

Every Sunday and feast day, after lunch, it was usual for the younger men of those hillsides and ravines to head up to Puiggraciós and the church with its hostel bar.

This was the meeting place at daybreak for those scattered worshippers of the district who had gone to early Mass when, every now and then, it was celebrated by some local priest or other. Later in the day, from noon through to the evening, it doubled as the haunt of card players intent on their game of *brisca* or *truc*. In the early morning what used to dominate the scene were the women's white headdresses, converging from all directions and going into the little church, summoned by the cracked sound of the bell which seemed to be saying, amid the silence of the woods around: *Up you come, dang, dang... Come up, please, dang...* Then, from late morning onwards, the place was taken over by males of all ages, some of them quite young, who, with a carnation tucked above one ear and cracking roasted pine nuts, went into the run-down hostel that was set like a buttress against the lower part of the church wall. The same pottering landlord who had assisted at morning Mass, wearing the surplice over his trousers, had now become the innkeeper who went to and from the wine barrel, collecting from his wife the glass pitchers with slender conical spouts after she had carefully filled them, and then delivering these *porrons* to the clients at the regular gathering: a shepherd or two, farmhands, charcoal burners or woodsmen turning up from who knows where…

It was now quite some time since Mass had been said in the church… but this did not mean that, on any Sunday afternoon, you would not find a sizeable crowd in the hostel bar, all playing at *truc* or *brisca* and draining glass after glass of wine.

Getting to the place was no problem at all for the people up at Ocata: a few good strides, and there they were. But the men who came from the far side of the Black Wood, or from beyond the ridge where the Romaní farm stood, had a long walk to make. There was a shepherd from even further away, from the hamlet of Vallcàrcara, who used to take a good hour between leaving home and showing his face at Puiggració… And then quite a few of them turned off from their direct route, making a deliberate detour, in order to drop down for a drink of water at the Fairy Spring, close to Rovira. Among all the springs thereabouts, most of them inhabited by mysteries and legends, the Fairy Spring was the one most renowned for its healing properties… The contingent who climbed by that route from around Uià never failed to make a stop here, even though the drop down into the deep gully where the water gushed out was tricky and even dangerous for anybody who was not completely sure of the way. While the visitor's feet were still on the poplar-clad ledge, there was no difficulty… but the rock chute which had to be negotiated next was so very tight, so damp and slippery, that one had to cling firmly to branches and thicket, in order to avoid crashing down to the dark bed of the ravine. The thing was that the waters of the Fairy Spring were famous for bringing benefit to all who drank there, preventing bad dreams and protecting against misfortune... And so it really was not right to pass that way without going down to take a drink of the miraculous water, or perhaps even just to wet one's fingers there and to cross oneself, as long as nobody else was standing close enough to see.

After doing this, it did seem that those who had performed the ritual now felt better, their spirit comforted. And then, once they had got out of that toad hole, darker and deeper than the shaft of any well, they cut back with a few bounds on to the main path and so continued up the mountain side until they reached the church at the top of the climb, from where they could survey all the sunlit plains of the Vallès area spreading down towards the south.

On that particular Sunday afternoon, a good number of people had gone up to Puiggraciós. But the charming sight of the lovely plains stretching away from beneath that elevated spot offered no attraction to the brutish denizens of the sombre ravines. They went glumly into the hostel bar, nodding distractedly as though they were going to a wake rather than to a place of amusement. The only greetings that they exchanged were vague acknowledgements:

'What do you know?'
'Can't complain...'
'Here we are, then...'
'Could be worse...'

And these words came from the most talkative among them, because the majority just kept their mouths shut, as though embarrassed to speak at all. Without saying even a single word most of them sat down around tables and then, by nodding or turning their head, ordered a drink from the hostel keeper's wife or set up a game of cards. So, even with a good many people gathered together in the smoke-stained rooms of the little hostel, what reigned there was a strange kind of stillness, interrupted only every now and then by the sound of a *porró* being put down on a table by the landlord, or by the short, sharp bids made by the card players:

'I'm calling!'

'Go on.'

'Three of a kind!'

'Full house!'

And the place fell back into a lifeless silence, as though the cloud of languor which floated eternally above them had thickened once again over those blear-eyed, confused men... As the wine flowed among the tables, with the *porrons* going the rounds, they became even more taciturn and inexpressive: their lives were depressing and their behaviour depressed, and so they tended to become maudlin in their cups. The more drink they gulped down, the more downcast and dour they became.

Then, all of a sudden, disturbing that oppressive atmosphere, a loud, gleeful voice rang out:

'Here I am! It's me!'

'Carbassot...' they all muttered at once, raising their heads as though waking up, while a shadowy likeness of mirth flickered over those dead faces from which any kind of real smile seemed to have been banished for ever.

Yes, indeed. It was young Carbassot, the swineherd from the Ensulsida farm, a squat, thickset young fellow who enjoyed a widespread reputation for the coarse and cloddish wisecracks that he never missed a chance to come out with. The witticisms of this woodland buffoon had the almost miraculous power of making the most uncouth shepherds and the fiercest foresters burst into fits of laughter. And then, on top of this, there were the pranks he got up to, at every turn, in order to frighten old women and to stir into panic people out and about in the deep valleys. One such jape was when, near to Romaní, a lifesize dummy dressed in men's clothes was discovered, horrifyingly strung up from the bough of a walnut tree... Approaching the scene, filled with dread, people exclaimed: 'Jesus, Mary and Joseph! Aleix has hung himself! Aleix has hung himself!'... only to discover that the corpse was just a bundle of old rags that the swineherd had tied up together to look like the twisted figure of the old man of Romaní. Or another time, in one stream bed or another, somebody would come across a man lying on the ground with a blanket round him, yelping and gasping as though in his death throes... and when the passer-by asked 'What's going on here? Hey, good man, what is wrong with you?' out of the blanket would spring Carbassot to go skipping away up the mountain side.

The swineherd from Ensulsida supplied the only fun, the only entertainment on offer to the folk who lived in the Montmany ravines, their only distraction. So when he turned up at the hostel the people there said, as though they had been missing him:

'We thought you weren't coming, Carbassot.'

'My sow was dropping her litter, so I had to go and fetch the woman who lends a hand,' replied the pig-keeper, giving rise to strange looks on the faces of those in the bar, who seemed to have the urge to laugh but didn't quite know at what.

And, although they were all by nature tight fisted and mean, he was immediately invited to drink with them, and also to join in a game of cards, with the idea of getting him to raise his elbow and to let fall some of his crude banter while calling trumps to those at his table.

'Here you are, Carbassot, have a drink… try some of this, it's got a real sting in its tail… and pick up your cards,' they said as they were making room for him in a group who were playing *bescambrilla*.

'What's the play?' the pig-man asked.

'Clubs are trumps.'

'Damn and blast!' was his response, 'Clubs are for hitting people with, like cudgels and staves, when there's a shindy.'

And he kept the whole gathering spellbound as he was slinging back his drink and delivering all his gab.

'Lead with trumps, Carbassot,' said his partner who was calling the play.

'Trumps? The best I can manage here is a fart…'

'Then go high… give it as much weight as you can.'

'Wait for a bit, and I'll just go up the cliff to see what I can find… unless the priest has been there already and taken most of the stone away for repairing the church and his own house…'

And how they all laughed… at least to the extent that those grim people were capable of laughter.

Meanwhile, night had begun to fall, and many were leaving the smoky rooms in the hostel, going their various ways over the Ocata ridge or heading silently down into the ravines. Even the ones who had swigged the most drink walked straight, looking serious, gloomy, just like when they had arrived.

But Carbassot, who did not hold his drink too well, went out with his head so cloudy that everything around him seemed to be unsteady and swirling. He almost had to grope his way through the darkness as he went down alone towards the hollow where Uià lay, staying as close as he could to the opposite side of the track from the steep drop down to the stream, nervous about slipping into it. He had the feeling that, as he stumbled along, some of the trees were bowing mockingly to him while others were performing a merry dance for his entertainment alone. 'Carbassot, you're sozzled!' the pig-man said under his breath. 'Carbassot, you're drunk!' Still feeling very dizzy, and now with a burning dryness in his throat, as he came close to Rovira, he thought: 'Just a minute... What about going down to the Fairy Spring? You could have a drink there, and freshen yourself up... and the water there is marvellous, so good for you, it might clear your head a bit.'

So, clutching at the stumps of holm oaks and patches of rosemary, he groped his way to find the opening which would take him down to the stream bed. He made good progress as he went through the poplars on the ledge, but then... as soon as he put one foot on to the steep rock of the narrow defile, he knew that he was in trouble, real trouble. His muddled thoughts suddenly cleared in the face of danger, and he would gladly have gone back upwards. However, turning himself around in that tight space would have been even more dangerous than carrying on straight down, so he took a step forwards. He tried to take another one... but he immediately felt that he had nowhere to plant his foot. He snatched desperately now at a clump of poisonous redoul, but the stems broke as he hung on to them... downwards he fell, rolling and tumbling, into the dark depths of the precipice.

When he crashed on to the stream bed, the pig-man let out a mortal scream which would have struck horror into the stoutest heart:

'Aaagh... I'm done for... I'm going to die!'

However, as no living soul was abroad in those parts, his cry of anguish was swallowed up in the eternal peace of the mountains, in the infinite serenity of the star-filled sky.

'I'm dying… dying!' He kept repeating in a loud, heart-rending voice which gradually turned into a groan of agony and despair, so feeble now and so deep in tone that it barely carried at all in the silence of the night.

'Aaagh! Aaagh!' he kept moaning at regular intervals, until close by there came two people who were the last to set off from the hostel at Puiggraciós. One was a cowherd from Uià and the other a lad from Ca l'Oliveres, walking back home in no particular haste, and they stopped to listen when they heard the howling that reached their ears.

'Do you hear that?'

'Aye…'

'Odds-on it's Carbassot…'

'You're right, it is.'

'I bet he wants to give us a fright.'

'Yeh, for sure.'

'He's such a joker…'

'Always pulling people's legs, winding them up!'

'Yes… but he's good at it…'

'He is, for sure.'

'Enough to make your sides split with laughing…'

'He'd even get corpses to have a laugh with him!'

And the two late revellers carried along their way, half smiling to themselves as they thought about that damned fellow, him and all his jesting…

After this some time went by, quite some time – a quarter of an hour, maybe half an hour – everything was enveloped in the deepest silence. And then, all of a sudden, there was the sound of leaves moving in the gap above the steep-sided defile. It was a rustling noise, gentle but sort of restless, like that which might have been made by the body of a person or an animal pushing its way through undergrowth. Finally, the thicket of juniper and gorse was parted by two sturdy arms to reveal the figure of Carbassot. He was dreadfully bruised, bedraggled and filthy.

'One slip and that would have been the end of me...' the swineherd grunted as he was running his hands over legs and shoulders to see how badly the bruises hurt.

Seen in the pale starlight, with his clothing ripped to shreds, his face covered in scratches, hair plastered on his forehead, the young man's puffed up, porky figure looked like some monster brought into being in the very bowels of the ravine.

'Bugger me! That was nearly curtains... and the next thing would be a call to the undertaker!' he kept moaning. 'And then those two bastards who came by this way, without even stopping to ask, "What's wrong with you, for God's sake?" One of these days I'll get my hands on you, and it'll be tit for tat...'

Then, suddenly, as though an idea had flashed through his mind, he let out a vigorous peal of laughter that resounded beyond the top of the Bertí cliffs.

'No sooner said than done! That's it!' the pig-man exclaimed, still laughing, 'This will be a good ruse alright!'

And returning sharply up the hillside, as if nothing had occurred, he was very soon back at Puiggraciós. The hostel was closed, and so he hammered furiously on the door: *thud, thud, thud.* 'Who's there?' somebody inside called out. 'The church here is on fire!' the swineherd shouted back, disguising his voice. By the time the hostel keepers had come outside, Carbassot was already at Can Coll: *thud, thud, thud* on the door! 'Who's there?' once more was the response. 'There's a fire in your loft!' And, as the people there were coming out, amid frightened shouts and the barking of dogs, the young fellow was now heading steeply downhill towards Rovira: *thud, thud, thud!* 'What's going on?' 'Your pine wood has caught fire!' And he did not stop until he reached the priest's house: 'There's a fire in the church!' And finally he beat on the door at Uià:

'Your straw ricks are burning!'

Everybody in the valley is at their wits end, with dogs barking and howling, sheep bleating, women screaming in fright, men shouting wildly, as though Judgement Day had come... And, while Carbassot has to clutch his belly, aching from laughing so much, the terrified people in the houses are calling out:

'The Devil himself has been let loose!'

VIII

The Church Refurbished

What a din, Lord! What noisy agitation went on around the priest's house during those five months and more that the building work on the church lasted! Everything became topsy-turvy, everything was shifted around and moved out of place... Not a hole was left unrepaired, every tiny corner was carefully checked over. In truth, through all the upheavals, that period of exhausting hard labour saw them all putting their backs into it... the priest with the fervour of an apostle... Mariagna and Josep with the obedience and resignation of humble servants... From daybreak until late at night, they were in constant movement, busily coming and going. Father Llàtzer had managed to bring up from Ametlla only two skilled craftsmen to work on the renovations, and he was lucky to get these. It meant that he and his aged companions had been obliged to be constantly on their toes helping the builders. While Mariagna was slaving away to provide home comforts and to do all their cooking, the priest and old Josep were fully occupied in labouring for them, erecting and taking down scaffolding, slaking lime for cement and then mixing the mortar, guiding pack animals over stone tracks to bring in materials or carrying up sand from the mill brook.

Driven by his desire to see the repairs to the church completed, the priest threw himself into every job that came his way, slaving away all day long, whether seeking timber for joists or going up through the woods in search of gravel from under the cliff... And, to see himself now, looking like the roughest simple country priest, sitting astride the mare in his bespattered cassock, he could not help thinking time and again back to his past, to those days of theological disputation when his writings had captivated both the wisest men and the gaping multitudes of a whole great city.

'If they could see me now, if they could see me looking like this...' he sometimes thought, his lips shaped in a vague smile that could have expressed either mockery or bitterness.

But any such inclinations to self-doubt quickly vanished as soon as he began to think how he, all on his own, without any helping hand from his parishioners, had found enough willpower to make life burst forth again in one small corner of that deep and dismal place where death seemed to reign. To think that he on his own had brought forth life, that he had brought all of this into being! He had not had to rely at all on the sluggish inhabitants of those hillsides... Rather than appealing again for help from those individuals who never looked anybody straight in the eye and who would never say a word, he had preferred to go knocking on the doors of people who were not part of their world. Inspired by faith and full of courage he had gone to seek help from devout residents who had no roots in the area, then from the dean of the whole district, from his good friends in the city. And, on returning to those cheerless ravines, after his pilgrimage to find support, he carried deep within his spirit not just the certainty that he was going to build once more the temple of God: he also bore there something perhaps even better… the hope of reviving his parishioners with that example of the church reborn, which would be a kind of miracle.

A hitherto unknown pleasure, the pleasure felt by a man who triumphs over obstacles and brings to fruition his own projects, now mysteriously delivered a thrill to his spirit every time he observed how, at his command, dormant places were being revived and dead things were acquiring the capability of movement. What delight, what strange, deep delight was felt by Father Llàtzer, like a saint performing miracles! And this feeling came to him as he sensed that, all around him, everything was coming back to life and brightening up to the pulsing of his own willpower, so that even the slack and slothful things which previously had been such grinding hindrances to him now showed signs of vigour.

That stubborn thick mat of grass which had impeded the way from the church to his house was now lying in loose bundles down in stream beds, leaving clear the paths between and around the buildings. Those square-hewn blocks which had fallen out of the walls, lying on the ground and getting in the way, had been lifted back to join in taking the strain of holding up the roof vaults. That poor church, gradually crumbling away, with its sinking flagstones, its walls full of cracks and its roofing open to the sky, was rising up once more, now more solid and strong, resolved to stand firm against the assault of centuries to come. Even the poor decaying building of the priest's house was joyfully raising its head again; for, once work on the church itself was completely finished, the house was partly renovated as well as could be. As the building was quite big enough for the few people who abided there, the most ruinous part of it was pulled down altogether, the rubble being used to reinforce the main entrance side, which was still more or less sound. And this new, tidily reduced dwelling was a delight to see, with its dazzling white walls, its red roof and its fresh green paint on the shutters! And then the flowerbeds, with their double violets and their rose bushes which the priest had arranged to be planted along the pathway leading to the vegetable patch!

Everything was flourishing, everything was smiling in that small, sad corner of the world... Everything resumed its function, everything was returning to life, reborn... everything, except the cloddish parishioners, who carried on, day and night, in their perpetual stupor, more dead to the world than their inanimate surroundings.

'The truth is that preaching or prayers have achieved nothing, absolutely nothing here!' the priest mused sadly. 'I have been able to jolt the stones hereabouts, but not to do anything to move these crude and dirty people. I have shifted boulders from where they stood, dragging them down the mountain to the church... but I have not had the strength to tear these woodlanders out of the eternal slumber that oppresses them. But now perhaps they will come back to life... and what could not be achieved by entreaties and kind words will henceforth be accomplished by tangible examples and deeds completed. When they see that out of the ruins the church has soared upwards again, on graceful new wings, they will all feel restored, with a will to live life fully again. Then I shall say to them, 'Look, just look at the poor old lady from centuries long ago, see how she is now decked out in new clothes, as though ready to go to a wedding! Look how she swings her brand-new door in the middle of the façade; how she shows off all the fresh proud pointing which runs from the entrance all the way round to the apse; look how she blinks with the stained glass in her windows; see how she holds her head high, with that bell tower built up again from its courses of stone that had been lying in a heap on the ground! And you, what can you do? You too can lift up your heads once more, raise your spirits, because for the church and for you the hour of resurrection has come!'

As the day for reopening the church to its parishioners approached, Father Llàtzer was becoming more and more confident that God would touch their hearts, so that, in the presence of the newly risen church, they would fall prostrate with admiration, as though before the radiance of a great prodigy.

The pity was that things were not completed as quickly as he would have liked. And the reason for this was that, once the building work was finished and the craftsmen had been paid off, the three inhabitants of the house had to set about cleaning from top to bottom the whole of the church interior. It was such a long and laborious chore, daunting for all of them. All the dust and powder from working the stone had fallen in white patches on the old black dirt which covered the floor, the product of centuries of neglect on the part of the woodlanders. It was necessary now to remove from the statues of saints and the altars themselves and from the holy vessels the layers of dust that covered everything, dust which grotesquely disguised the true colours and shapes of each single item. A thorough brushing was needed to remove the new dust which had quickly gone to settle in hidden nooks and crannies, as though resisting capture. It was necessary also to bring down the black cobwebs which clung high up in the rafters like clusters of sleeping bats. Then there were the thick patches of mould, like a rash covering the columns, panels and tracery of the altar screens, which had to be carefully cleaned off... And it was such hard work to remove all that dank, stale residue which had been patiently tended over long years by the venerable ministration of dead centuries. The filth seemed to be at home there, drowsing in corners and cracks. When they removed it from one place, it quickly fled to snuggle somewhere else. Momentarily disturbed, flecks of dust flew around everywhere like tiny malign imps, until they fell asleep again once they had landed in a new place...

Then there began a long, undignified tussle between the dust, which settled everywhere, and the priest with both of his aged companions who pursued it with committed patience. Scrubbing, wiping and washing, working in silent concentration through every corner of the temple, it seemed that the three of them were performing a quite unwonted ceremony of purification. It took on the character of a strange ritual cleansing, a kind of exorcism to rid the church of the evil spirits idly lingering or drowsing in the dust. Mariagna in particular, with her air of dumb resignation, so long-suffering and inexpressive, as though she had taken a vow of humility and silence, went thoroughly over each of the altars, one panel at a time, cleaning the candlesticks and lampstands one by one, just as if she were following to the very letter the complicated rules of some mysterious rite. 'Away with you!' she seemed to be saying, in a kind of muttered prayer, to the grime that lurked in the embossing and in cracks. 'Away with you, all you bone idle dust! Get up, get moving and get on your way in the name of God! Away with you damned cobwebs! Go and get spun in the pine trees out in the woods! Off you go, tiresome fluff! Outside with you this instant, and don't let us see you ever again!'

And so Mariagna went about her duty, in an attitude of complete devotion, making many reverential bows and crossing herself at each altar... and with her feather duster in her hand, as though it were the aspergillum, she ceremonially made to despatch the filth from the sacred objects, driving it out for a bracing walk far from the house of the Lord...

Church of Sant Pau de Montmany, Rovira farm and the Bertí cliffs.
(Courtesy of Salvador Llobet/the Municipal Archive, Granollers)

IX

The Bells Ring Out

When the day arrived for Mass to be celebrated for the first time since completion of the building work, the church was gleaming like a mirror. The freshly washed white cloths on all the altars, the glossy decoration on the frames of the altar cards, and the candlesticks holding their new candles, all together formed the impression of a fine bunch of flowers. The high altar could not have looked more splendid. The braid on the canopy, the moulding on the steps, the scallops decorating the niches, cornices and side panels… everything shone as though freshly regilded. Curly heads of little cherubs smiled from the bases and the capitals of the columns, looking at the hanging bunches of golden grapes that were entwined along the twists of the pillars. The figures of the saints, previously so knocked about and shabby, had been brought back from death into life. All the images were clothed in carefully repaired tunics and neatly darned capes, like rustic saints, poor but well turned out. Saint Isidore's dangling arm had been put back in place, repaired and now resting again on his hoe; Saint Sebastian, freshly repainted, stood tightly bound to the tree trunk where he was martyred, with the arrows in his flesh resilvered; and Saint Paul, the stocky patron saint of the parish, thundered out his message from the stand in the centre of the high altar.

Overcome with joy, the priest was beside himself with expectation, impatiently anticipating the time for the bells to ring calling his parishioners to prayer and for them to be shown that gift from God which was sure to work the miracle of bringing them back to life. Long before daylight he was already going back and forth in the church, putting the finishing touches to the altarpieces. In order to see how wonderful the high altar would look when it was all illuminated, he did a rehearsal by lighting tapers and candles on the side table, on the steps, in the niches and along the edge of the cornice... And when it was all lit up, when the altar was resplendent with so many twinkling points of brightness, shining, burning, glowing, sparkling like a golden brazier, the priest felt half-forming on his lips some words which were probably inspired by the Bible and which always came to him whenever hope and joy sprang forth in his heart: *'The way of the temple had been effaced, and the people had forgotten its ceremonies; but I have raised up the ruins of the house of the Lord and have lit the lamps in the tabernacle...'*

Then he awoke from that ecstasy which had possessed him for an instant, and he once more started giving orders to the old couple, as though to use in some constructive way the time which was dragging painfully before the sun would rise and before Mass would begin.

'Josep!'

'Father...'

'Start laying out the ornaments and my vestments, ready for the service. You've already put everything in the sacristy, haven't you? The amictus, the alb and its ribbon?'

'Yes, Father.'

'And you, Mariagna, go to the garden and pick all the roses you can find… Make up some bunches and we shall put them in the vases… I want the altar to have a lot of flowers on it.'

'Very well, Father.'

And as soon as he saw the brightness of morning coming up behind the terraces at Uià, he could restrain himself no longer.

'Come along, Josep, the time has come. Go and give the bells a good airing!'

But, no sooner had he given the order than he immediately had second thoughts, saying to himself: 'No, no! Josep would not be capable of ringing them properly… He is a good man, uncomplaining, obedient… but insensitive, simple-minded, doltish… He has neither the soul nor the spirit to make the bells speak as I want them to…'

'No, Josep, don't you go,' he said to the old man, who was just starting to climb the steps up to the belfry. I want to ring them myself… I shall make them say what they have to say…'

And as he climbed the stairs, in a state of illumination, transfigured, as though seized by inspiration, he was murmuring quietly to himself: 'They have stayed silent for too long, the poor bells! Now that they have got their voices back, they must speak forth with a triumphant sound… they must intone such a chant of glory as was never heard before… a kind of hallelujah which will be a hymn of praise to the Lord for having allowed me to rebuild the church… and a loud awakening call to the slumbering people of the woods…'

And up he went briskly to the top of the steps, as the old man was coming back down, humbly. Once in the belfry, the first thing the priest did was to make the sign of the cross, praying for God to inspire him. Then he eagerly grasped the rope of the big bell… and, feeling the counterweight only just jerking into a slight movement despite all his heaving, he was struck by a sudden dismay… 'Mercy on us! What if the bell was not now able to chime, after such a long time without being rung…' But he gave the rope one more really strong tug, and then, making a single full turn on its mounting, the bell spoke forth: *Dong*… 'Thanks be to God, thanks be to God!' Then one more heave… and the great bronze artefact, turning comfortably now, began to sing majestically: *Dong… dong… dong…* 'That's it! That is it!' thought Father Llàtzer, filled with joy. 'This is the *Te Deum* of which I had dreamed for celebrating the poor church's resurrection!' *Dong… dong… dong…* 'Thanks be to you, good Lord, great thanks!' *Dong… dong… dong…*

But then the priest suddenly remembered that his main duty was to awaken his slumbering parishioners, his dead parishioners, with a joyful peal to stir their spirits, to brush away their drowsiness, to lift from them the dead weight under which they lay… And, turning to the smaller bell, he grasped its clapper with one hand and began the most rapid, repeating peal that he could manage: *Ding, ding-ding! Ding, ding!* 'Come on, come on now; stir yourselves, you dwellers in darkness!' said the priest, as though to add emphasis to the voice of the bells. *Ding, ding-ding! Ding, ding!* 'And come along, all of you, right away!' *Ding, ding-ding! Ding, ding!* 'And you shall see the miracle of the church that has come back to life…' *Ding, ding-ding! Ding, ding!*

Then Father Llàtzer stopped for a while, and looking out through the belfry window, he tried to see if the ravines were awakening. But… everything was silence and solitude. The last wisps of shadow were slipping away from the deepest nooks, to be replaced by the first patches of morning mist weaving in and out of the pine trees or dispersing in the air. But of living beings... there was no sign. Not a sign nor a shadow. This was when the priest decided that he must redouble his own effort and the call of the bells, and he began then to sound a peal with both clappers at once. It was a desperate clangour made to bring souls towards eternal life. *Dong! Dong! Ding, ding, ding! Dong, dong! Ding, ding!*

However, despite the desperate pealing of the bells, there was still no sign of life from the people, and the priest, with his hope very nearly gone, disillusioned and drained, began to ring out the call to Mass, unhurriedly now. Those initial, anxious wake-up calls were replaced by the deliberately idling triple sequence: *Dong... dong... dong!* And it was that measured appeal which worked the miracle...

When Father Llàtzer looked out again through the belfry window, he felt his heart beginning to swell. From the half-ruined houses of the ravines white scarves and long black shawls were beginning to come out and, like corpses in shrouds emerging from tombs, they were making their way very steadily towards the church. The priest raised his eyes heavenwards, because he believed that the hour of resurrection had arrived.

Lunch at La Rovira.
(Courtesy of Josep Vilardebò i Puig)

X

Bad Stock!

Dong... That first single chime from the church belfry resounded through the shadowy ravines like some mysterious word that could not be properly understood. The bells had been silent for so long that, when they now sent forth this initial call, it was as though they were tongue-tied, like a child first beginning to babble. Then, however, on the second strike, *Donnng...* the bronze voice became clearer, and soaring upwards, it flew and carried strongly, spreading everywhere, way over the cliff tops and into the deepest recesses of every gorge. Each measured strike of the big bell was like a fresh breath of life, warm, gentle, affectionate, which was gradually going to thaw the torpor of nights eternal.

But that was nothing compared with the effect achieved next by the smaller bell... As soon as its joyful clamour broke out, then everything was quickly enlivened. Enervated grass festooning the ditches suddenly stirred, shaking off the dewdrops. From shrubs and bramble patches birds emerged in flocks, squawking and twittering, alarmed by the clangour from the bell tower. The thickest parts of the dismal woods, deadened by somnolence and cold, were being probed by the tremulous ringing sound which seemed to rub up against the trees and to tickle their leaves, as though deliberately trying in this way to arouse feeling in the inert, numbed trunks and the mist-shrouded branches.

Then the merry pealing climbed higher, ever higher, going up towards the cliff tops, the hills and the crags, until they crowned with a joyful noise the whole circle of dark mountains walling in the hollow from which the sound arose. And when the lively fanfare arrived as far as the tumbledown hamlet on the other side of the pass above Ocata, everybody was perplexed by the uplifting sound. The people there stretched their arms and rubbed their eyes, like corpses being roused on hearing the trumpet of Judgement Day.

The old woman at Can Pugna muttered, as she strained to hear:

'I don't know if I'm hearing things or dreaming... but I think they're ringing the church bells.'

Over on the opposite hillside, the girl who looked after the pigs at Rovira shouted out in surprise:

'Don't you hear, master, don't you hear? Listen how the bells are chiming!'

The blind farmer at Uià put his head out of the window in order to hear better the stirring sound.

Disturbed by that restless music of bells, which seemed to be announcing urgently the resurrection of the flesh and the promise of eternal life, the woodsmen did not know what to do nor what to decide upon. It was so long since they had set foot inside the parish church that they were extremely reluctant to go down there. Ever since the day that the new priest had called them to gather in the cemetery, in order to preach to them about the sacred duty of repairing the buildings, not one of them had shown their face anywhere near the place. If ever they had to travel from one side of the parish to the other, rather than going by the church buildings they chose to go the long way round, cutting across the slopes near the Sunyer farm or going right round along the foot of the cliff. All this was from fear of bumping into that crazed priest who wanted to stir them into action and drag them out of the quietude of their sleepy mountains. So how uncomfortable, how embarrassing it now was to think about going back to the church, freshly repaired from top to bottom, no thanks at all to them! And how the new priest would smirk, as though reminding them that he had not had any need at all of his parishioners' help.

Then, while they were still wrestling anxiously with this uncertainty about what to do, what to say... suddenly the frantic chiming of the small bell ceased and the big bell began to ring out slowly the call to Mass: *Dong... Dong... Dong...* Whereupon men and women from the woods were jerked into motion, and as though obeying a stern order of the kind that cannot be quibbled about or contradicted, they all reluctantly got ready to go down into the ravine, with dejected and resigned looks on their faces. The men, as though mechanically, took down from pegs their outdoor wraps and capes, while the women brought out their headwear from settle drawers. There was nothing else for it... Those three resonant, regular strokes were a command whose observance had been handed down from fathers to sons through centuries and centuries. There was nothing else for it... They had to lower their heads, resign themselves and set off downhill. What they were obeying was not so much the voice of the Lord, transmitted by the bell, as the law of timeless custom, passed down from generations of yore. They were doing what their parents before them had done, what their grandparents had done, what all their ancestors had done, way back through the most distant centuries. There was nothing else for it... It was like the nightly course of the stars in the sky, like the changes of the earth's seasons: something which cannot be rebelled against. They all had to bow their heads at the pealing which rang out from the belfry, in the same way that they submitted to the heat of the sun and the chill of the night, to rain and to fine weather, to darkness and to light. Nothing else for it... No way of answering back... So on their way down to the church, they looked pensive and worried as they went through the woods, inwardly resentful while outwardly meek, like sheep driven along by blows from the stout stick of a tough domineering shepherd. They went one step at a time, but they were moving along... Come on now, on you go! With scarves on their heads or capes around their shoulders, they looked like tormented souls who, having been brought out of limbo, were condemned to follow a route which they dreaded, like it or not...

The first of the woodlanders who eventually reached the church were quite taken aback, and then vexed, when they looked on all the work that had been done.

'What's been going on?' they muttered. 'What's all this?'

And torn between surliness and the urge to snoop closer, through dim eyes they inspected all those parts of the building which had been renovated, all those sleeping corners which had miraculously woken up, all those dead things which had now come back to life. Old and young frowned with noses wrinkled, as though they were having difficulty taking in the breath of life and the freshness given off by those lovely surroundings which, until quite recently, had lain neglected and crumbling. They looked here, there and everywhere, as though conducting an investigation; they moved two steps forwards, and then turned and came back again... How they peeked and pried, with snide comments at every end and turn. And the more they looked and the more they snooped, the greater became their peevishness and their sullenness. That once decrepit church, now younger and stronger than ever; that little house where the priest lived, now with its brilliant white walls; that little garden plot, now in such bloom; those paths now so tidily cleared: all these things filled their gaze, affecting them like mockery or taunts. Temple, house, garden, paths, all basked in their own joyful triumph and smiled. And the more they smiled to display their triumph, the more the parishioners were enraged and discomforted, to the point of imagining that they themselves were being scoffed at by everything they beheld, as though everything was making faces at them and saying to taunt them: 'So there! So you parishioners thought – did you? – that without your help we could never raise our heads again? Well, now you can see... We have had no need at all of you. The new priest, who is a saint of a man, has brought us back to life, all on his own, by himself! What do you think of that, what do you think?'

And the rustic flock, with befuddled heads still turning over and over their misgivings and suspicions, were ever more quickly becoming inwardly and darkly enraged, to the point of bursting. They felt humiliated, ridiculed: and such was their bewilderment, that finally, all the resentment they felt towards the priest showed itself in their eyes and came out through their words.

'Just look at him, the bleedin' priestman,' one of them said, 'and how he's managed to get the church repaired!'

'I don't know how he's been able to do it, the sly old scoundrel!'

'Didn't I always tell you that this one's a crafty blighter?'

'Blast his eyes! I reckon he's in league with the Devil...'

'For sure, for bloody sure! All this has the look of black magic about it...'

The conversation ended there, because at that very moment a cry of anguish was heard, a half-choked... 'My God!' that silenced them all. Nobody could tell where that pained exclamation came from. The woodsmen turned round, but could not see anyone howling or moaning close to where they were.

It was Father Llàtzer, poor man, who had looked from behind the cypresses in the graveyard to see with his own eyes the working of the miracle of his dead parishioners coming back to life. He it was who had stifled that tortured cry on hearing what was being said.

His hopes of redemption had suddenly melted away, as if they had all disappeared deep underground. The scowling innermost being of his primitive parishioners had been disclosed right in front of him, in all its cragged and brutish nakedness. He had dreamed that they were gloomy presences wandering aimlessly through the woodland shadows, as incapable of doing good as of doing evil... But now he saw that he had indeed been dreaming, merely dreaming such things... He now understood that drowsy simpletons they might be, but they harboured sinfulness behind that dozy exterior. They did evil furtively, neither fully asleep nor fully awake, stealthily and quietly, without drawing attention... They did as much evil as they could, as long as this did not trouble their minds too much or disturb the torpor of their plodding existence... Any fine human quality had been bred out of them all! Bad stock, that's what they were!

Thereupon Father Llàtzer went and stood before them, with

a stern look on his face, gesturing like a prophet possessed by a saintly rage, determined to put them to shame, to execrate them, to lash their faces with harsh words that would decry such great iniquity, such baseness!

But the gathering of peasants dispersed in all directions as soon as they caught sight of the priest carried away by that fury. Some turned and moved towards the apse; others went inside the church, pretending they had noticed nothing. Some looked away so as not to have to greet the new priest… Others eyed him hesitantly, with a look partly of mockery and partly of stupidity… Father Llàtzer walked past all of them and, fighting hard to suppress the holy rage which inflamed his heart, he just murmured to himself, 'Bad stock!' He entered the church, crossed the nave and went into the sacristy, struggling all the while to quieten the tumult of indignation that was making his very soul shudder.

'It is not pious concern,' he said to himself, 'it is not compassion that needs to be given to these people who are rougher than the land they work, more darkly treacherous than the black of night… What will yoke them and keep them in submission is a vision of chastisement, the preaching of the message of eternal torment…' He was going over and over these ideas as he went to the chest where his ceremonial garb was kept.

But as soon as he looked at the holy vestments, he felt terrified by his own thoughts. As soon as he had picked up the amictus robe to place it over his shoulders, he remembered that this cloth was the mystical veil with which Christ's eyes were covered when he was being mocked and insulted… and he began to feel comforted by that memory of divine patience. Next, when he pulled the tunic over his head, he felt further consoled, reflecting that the white garment was the madman's

103

clothing in which the Son of Man was dressed on the night of his Passion. When this was done, as he tied the alb ribbon, he had become almost completely calm, because through his mind were passing visions of the ropes that bound His hands in the Garden of Gethsemane and the lashing He received in the praetorium...

But then, suddenly, as he was about to cross over his chest the two ends of his golden stole, the sign of immortality and the majestic attribute of his ministry, the flames of indignation that burnt within him began, without his understanding why, to surge up once more in his head.

'Bad stock,' he kept repeating, unable to prevent himself. 'Bad stock! Like Caesar's henchmen, they also are mocking Christ and treating him like a madman! They ascribe to the Devil the work of God, and they take miracles for witchcraft! They are just like the old tribes of the Jews, spitting their ingratitude towards Heaven! They want to know nothing of a God of love... they set themselves against the God who performs acts of eternal justice! Instead of a priest administering the law of Grace, what they need is one to dispense the ancient laws, to make them feel the weight of divine ire, to call down on them the fires of Heaven, to damn them even unto the fourth generation!'

Such was the indignation he felt towards the uncouth and benighted peasants that he was on the point of divesting himself of his holy garments, of going to the presbytery and ordering that the church be shut, shouting: 'Go away, leave this place! You can all go away right now! There will be no Mass for the depraved!' But, making a supreme effort, he once more reined in his powerful feelings and finished putting on the vestments, ready to go towards the altar. Filled with unction, with a deeply contemplative look, his head bowed and his eyes closed, his lips trembling in prayer, the priest went out of the sacristy, with one hand holding the chalice and the other upon the cloth covering the communion bread and wine.

But once he was in the gaze of his congregation, as he went from the sacristy to the presbytery, he turned his head all of a sudden, as though stirred out of his meditation by the irreverent noise that drifted towards him from the nave. The folk gathered there were creating that confused sound with their shuffling and loud whispers… They were muttering into each other's ear, making signs one to another, pointing at the freshly painted altars, the restored images and fittings… Then Father Llàtzer stopped for a moment, facing his parishioners, and quickly composing himself, motionless, in a stately severe pose, like a statue of divine majesty, he glared long and hard at the throng, with a look so dazzlingly intense that it brought those men and women to their knees. A sepulchral silence suddenly came over the place… and intoning the celebratory prayer he went up to the altar.

What could there have been in that look and that pose of the priest which so stunned the peasants? Had they seen passing before their eyes the august image of the God to whom offence had been done, of the irate God, in the guise he will surely display when he comes to judge the quick and the dead on the dark day of Last Judgement? Something of this there must have been in their reaction… The fact was that, before seeing him holding the sacred ornaments, whether they had come across him close by his house or met him out in the woods, their attitude towards the new priest was invariably one of rancour and hostility, or else of mockery and disdain! But now, changed to say Mass, dressed in the cassock, with the chalice in his hand, standing at the foot of the altar… now that was something different, something really tremendous! At that moment they looked upon him as the minister of the God who holds in his powerful hands the storm and the hailstones, the snow and the ice, the lightning and the blasting wind, the diseases which afflict flocks and herds, the deaths of men and of animals!

Such insights into the dark spirit of the woodlanders went back and forth in the priest's head, while he was removing the cover from the chalice and then leafing through the missal.

'Is not the fear of God the beginning of everything?' he sighed. 'So might I still lead them to God through fear…'

And a ray of hope shone in his eyes as he said, now standing before the altar step:

'Introibo ad altare Dei.'

XI

The Story of the Old Couple

One of the other things which most afflicted Father Llàtzer, among the tragedies besetting him, was to find no consoling refuge in the old couple who were his servants. In them he found abundant, even excessive, respect, humility, veneration, but that was all. What he needed and was missing was affection. He could have done with a little less reverence and a little more emotional closeness. Living as he did in solitude in that mountain wilderness, separated from human contact, he would have welcomed it with heartfelt gratitude, as the best gift that Heaven could bestow, if the old couple, instead of venerating him as their lord and master, could have treated him like a son, or like a brother. A modicum of this kind of family warmth would have done a lot to bring him out of the chilly solitude to which he was condemned by his surly parishioners.

Every time that he returned home pained in mind and spirit by the consistent malevolence shown by the woodlanders – whether by their cutting off from a track in order not to have to greet him, or by putting on a sour face when they could not avoid meeting him – he would have preferred to see a tear of pity in the eyes of his obsequious companions rather than listen to that litany of *Yes, Father... No, Father* which was never far from their lips. For the priest it would have been real consolation if, whenever they saw him looking sad, downhearted because of the distress caused to him by people in the parish, they could have rushed to ask him what was wrong, what was upsetting him... And he would have told them, in one-to-one confidence, keeping it in the family as it were... the three of them might even have shed tears together, and so they would have done something to help heal the wounds that bled in his very soul... But they did no such thing. They were so obliging, so obedient, so overflowing with subservience that they could never find the kind word that was needed in a moment of affliction.

In order to get necessary things done, to fulfil their duties, both Mariagna and Josep would often go to extreme lengths of self-denial... and the most admirable thing was that they did this without realising it, as though it was nothing, as though what they did had no merit. Whether in household work, or in the service of the church, they never complained at all. They put their backs into every job: not just their backs, but their arms and legs, their physical strength and their senses... But they never put any true feeling into what they did. It was as though their hearts, through showing so much submission and respect, had been reduced to a condition in which any real tenderness of inward emotion had been turned into mere humility.

And thus the poor priest, by his nature so sociable and warm-hearted, found himself condemned to live in perpetual loneliness... Solitary, like an exile, when he walked through the ravines, surrounded by the black mountains; solitary and menacing like God in his divine anger, when he was in church, confronting his sullen congregation; solitary and revered, like a *sanctum sanctorum*, when he was at home in the company of his two servants. He certainly tried hard to win them round by speaking frankly to them; he did what he could to break down that wall of veneration which prevented the old couple from approaching him freely. But all his efforts were in vain. They, poor things, did not know how to behave any differently. In order to change their attitude they would have had to turn into different people, and they were far too old to become anything other than what they were. A whole life of servitude spent in the shadow of the cloister had moulded their spirit and their bodies according to the rules of the strictest discipline, inculcating in them that faded and withdrawn air of submission. The story of the old couple was a very strange one...

Josep was born and bred in Montmany itself, and he still remembered very well the time when, as a young child, he would roam his local hillsides and vales, one day assisting at Mass in the church and then the next running from house to house to recite psalms and paternosters in order to be able to help provide for his parents, both of them almost invariably afflicted by some illness or other. The poor mite had been born at Can Saborit, a dark and run-down little cottage which stood above the Can Ripeta col, and which was now, and for some years had been, a heap of rubble, totally deserted. It was there that, more often hungry than properly fed, the young lad grew up, passive and glum, watching as the little family home gradually crumbled and seeing how his parents were wilting and growing weaker, worn down by grinding poverty. Indeed, so weakened and ground down were they that eventually they died... And then the youngster, before the house finally collapsed about him, decided to leave those parts to see if he could earn his meagre daily bread in any other place where starvation was less likely. He made his way, with hardly any deviation, south towards Les Planes: and there, after much dogged perseverance, he arrived one day at the door of a large nunnery, where he begged for alms in God's name.

The poor young lad stood in awe at the sight of that immense religious building, almost as big as an entire settlement and with the look more of a palace than of a convent. Coming as he did from a poky, ruinous hovel, he could hardly take in the grandeur of the row after row of living quarters, all those yards, wine cellars and guest rooms, all so clean and tidy, so spacious, so bright and airy, located all around the enclosed space. But what filled him with even more wonder than anything else was the sight of the abbess walking in the main cloister, followed by her nuns, a magnificent and majestic presence, like a triumphant queen surrounded by a court of princesses in white. The poor little fellow was overcome with wonder, unable to take in all that abundant splendour.

As he was such a lanky, sinewy youth and had such a mystical and benign look about him, the nuns told him that, if he wanted to stay on, they did indeed need a lad to help the gardeners. He agreed to this, and from then on he never left the staff quarters of the convent. He was so obliging, so hard-working and straightforward, that he quickly became everybody's assistant, messenger or servant. 'Send for Josep', 'Tell Josep to do that', 'Get Josep to go there'. And he performed all his duties, humbly, devoutly, respectfully, whether the instructions came from the nuns or from the male servants or the maids in the convent.

From among the maids he got to know Mariagna, another orphan like himself, as contrite and simple as him, a girl who had also been taken in by the nuns. Among her duties was that of looking after the cattle; but, because she was so young and feeble, very often she was unable, despite all her efforts, to impose her will on the herd which would go wandering off in the gorges and stream beds. But then it was Josep who would rush to help her, and between them they would bring the beast back in, together they would change their bedding and together they would give them fodder. Although they spent so much time in each other's company, and despite being a couple of young people, they were always politely distant with one another, showing a kind of mutual respect that might have been expected among more civilised individuals. Whether out in the grounds, or in the staff quarters or in the convent itself, whenever they met the greeting was the same:

'God be with you, Mariagna.'

'God be with you, Josep'

And all the other servants in the convent were quite bemused and unable to withhold their smiles on hearing how politely that snotty-nosed pair addressed one another.

Then, one day, they found themselves by chance alone in the locutory, where they had gone to be given their orders, and the mother superior, who had noticed how alike they were in both character and bearing, said to them in an absent-minded sort of way:

'You two would make a good couple… You ought to get married…'

Whereupon the two young people, who had never ever dreamed of anything of the sort nor had ever exchanged more than the occasional word, replied straight away, in unison:

'Yes, Mother,' as if taking as a commandment those words that were still hanging in the air.

And so it came to pass. Shortly afterwards they were married, without their changed state bringing about any change at all in their habitually submissive and self-sacrificing behaviour. As time went on, their lives became even more staid, more taciturn, more devoted to the service of God and to the service of the convent. They treated one another with the same respect as before, with the same reserve and the same formality...

'I say, Mariagna...'

'What can I do for you, Josep?'

They were so modest and withdrawn in their life together that they seemed not so much husband and wife as brother and sister who had secretly made vows of obedience, poverty and chastity, just like the nuns themselves. The cloistered atmosphere in which they had lived and breathed for so long had instilled in them, over time, a certain way of bearing themselves, certain monkish gestures, that showed through in everything they did... in how they walked, in how they dressed, in how they expressed themselves. Although they were simple country people, they gave the impression of being completely at home in the convent, more like members of a religious order than sons of the soil. And this is how their lives were lived, for countless years and years, until they reached old age... which was when Father Llàtzer got to know them, after he had been ordered by his prelate to spend a month in penance at Les Planes, before undertaking his journey into the backwoods of Montmany.

'That's where I come from, Father, Montmany is in my part of the world,' said Josep one day, talking with the troubled priest.

And Father Llàtzer, on hearing those words, thought that it was a miraculous message which now offered him a way of getting through the adversity of his situation. He was lost in thought for a good while, reflecting that, if the old man were willing to accompany him on his pilgrimage, it would be like having a guide sent to him from Heaven. The part of the country to which he was being transferred was unknown terrain for him, and the idea of going there filled him with anxiety. He had heard it talked about as the back of beyond, a terrifying place all blanketed in mists, shadows and sadness; as a kind of dark limbo where people lived their lives as though in a death-like slumber. 'If I could at least go there accompanied by a good soul like this old man and a good woman like Mariagna,' he thought, 'then exile in those dark vales would perhaps not be so desolate or so cruel...'

Father Llàtzer was suddenly encouraged by that thought which had shone like a tiny flicker of starlight amid so much darkness in his mind, and he hurried to the nunnery to explain to the mother superior all the anxiety that burdened him and the one last shred of hope that he now had.

'If only I could take the dear old couple with me! If only they would be willing to come with me!'

And finally taking pity on him in his tribulation, the mother superior called the old couple to her presence. She began with gentle insinuation and then gradually implanted in their minds the priest's desire. But Josep and Mariagna did not have to be treated with so much delicate precaution: they were so accustomed to perpetual obedience and eternal submission, that as usual, they took her initial insinuation as a fully formed and explicit order, and with one voice they replied:

'Yes, reverend mother. As soon as it pleases your reverence, we shall depart.'

And from that moment on they set about getting everything prepared for the sad pilgrimage, fully resigned to abandoning the sunlit walls and the flower-bedecked cloisters where their lives had been spent, ready now to set off on the journey into the deep, dark wilderness. During the whole time they were travelling, on a route as rough and steep as Calvary itself, they never gave out a single sigh of sadness or a single moan of regret… And once they had arrived at their destination, once they were holed up in that lonely corner where they were to live as exiles from the world of men, neither of them had any other thought but of moulding to their new situation the habits they had followed in the convent. Absolutely nothing had impinged on the perpetually long-suffering spirits of the old couple. Everything was still done in the same way and at the same rhythm. The unremitting, silent labour; the habitual patience and self-sacrifice; and the God-be-with-you incessantly repeated in the convent: none of this behaviour was interrupted in the slightest. When, at midday or in the evening, their tasks completed, they briefly came together in the house, husband and wife would greet one another with the usual convention:

'May God be with you, Mariagna.'

'And with you forever, Josep.'

Once these words of greeting had been exchanged, each of them sank back into uninterrupted silence and like shades of persons from centuries past, they meekly went off again to their respective chores. The local people, seeing them coming and going in the vicinity of the church, silent and withdrawn like penitents in the wilderness, stared at them in bemusement and often even made fun of how they looked and behaved. Although the old couple dressed much the same as everybody else, there was something oddly ecclesiastical about how their clothes had been put on and were worn. Josep went about in a black smock which, had it been only a little longer, might have been a cassock; and with his arms crossed in their usual

114

position, with each hand tucked into the opposite oversleeve, he looked strangely, from any angle, like an ordained cleric. And as for Mariagna, it was even more obvious… She had a particular way of fastening under her chin the white scarf she wore as though it were a toque, and of putting on top of this her black hood, tipped forward so that it looked like a veil and so that she had all the appearance of being a real nun.

Father Llàtzer could not look at them without being struck that they could have been holy people from earlier centuries, forgotten survivors preserved in the here and now, or faded images that had escaped from an ancient reredos. What grieved him was that those quaint altar-saints, so perfectly self-denying and humble, did not bear within their habits a compassionate spirit that might have shown some real feeling for all the suffering he was experiencing. But they offered no such solace… far from it! What they saw in Father Llàtzer, as well as their lord and master, was the clergyman, God's minister, the priest… and that ministry, the dignity of that office, filled them with reverence and overwhelming respect. The real pity was that they were unable to recognise the man, the man of flesh and blood, who more than anyone else on earth needed to be comforted and to be shown compassionate feeling, there in that sepulchral wilderness in which he lived, condemned to suffer the ill will and the taunts of his scowling parishioners.

And he needed it there and then… never more urgently now that the silent hostility, the furtive warfare waged against him by the woodlanders from the start, seemed to be building up to a head in open confrontation! Without his knowing how, nor from which direction, he could feel a storm of rancour gathering over his head, about to burst, as impalpable as dark shadows, as basely treacherous as the black of night. He knew that they had a fierce grudge against him, and that the day of their villainy was at hand. The good thing was that he was not afraid, even so, of what lay in store; and encouraged by the mightiness of what his ministry signified, he was standing firm and ready to face the onslaught of his vicious neighbours. Indeed sometimes he even felt impatient for events to take their course, perhaps trusting that out of the very upheaval there would come about change, the new life, the redemption that he longed for…

Ever since the day when, holding the chalice and robed for saying Mass, he had seen his parishioners trembling from head to foot, terrified by the hard stare of indignation with which he was fixing them, he had harboured the hope of being able to use fear as a means of leading towards God that stubborn herd. So whenever one of them strayed from the straight and narrow and created an embarrassing scene, he knew how to choose his moment to impose discipline… He waited until the Sabbath and the hour for Mass, and then, when his whole congregation was gathered before the altar…, he would turn to face them and would reprimand the guilty person with angry words: 'You there, the boy from Ensulsida! Do you not fear God's punishment? I declare that you are quite heartless to behave as you do, letting your old mother go out begging in order to support you! And you over there, shepherd from Uià! I cannot understand why you don't crumble with shame for singing those lewd songs of yours when you are out in the woods and someone comes by, with you singing them out loud to be sure that they hear you! Do you not realise that God is also listening, and that with a bolt of his thunderous ire he can silence you for ever?'

And then they all bowed their heads beneath the weight of

the holy wrath. On hearing those reproaches delivered by the priest from the altar step, the parishioners were struck with fear and trembling; all of them, young and old, resolved, at least for a short time, to return to the path of righteousness and to obey God's command.

But the really distressing part of all this was that the priest's own heart bled when he had to chastise those people with such rage. He was all goodness and love, and his heart was rent every time that, from before the altar, he had to hurl at his flock the harsh words of execration. After having uttered his dire warnings like some exasperated prophet, he felt weak and faint. And Father Llàtzer would spend days and days in a state of lassitude and dejection, as though overwhelmed by the terror of his own powerful reprimands.

It was in those moments of extreme helplessness that the priest would have welcomed on bended knee some solace from his aged servants. To see a tear in their eyes, to hear a sigh coming from them... But it was not to be, not from those two... Always silent, always respectful, always so formally polite, they responded to Father Llàtzer's exclamations as though saying amen at the end of a prayer.

'You can see what I am going through! You can see my anguish!' the priest would exclaim with his head in his hands.

'Yes, Father,' was the only response they made, in a humble tone but one which was so faint and indistinct that they could have been a thousand leagues away.

The priest simply could not resign himself to the effects of the frosty reverence of that old couple, as faithful as family dogs, as submissive as slaves, but as tightly shut as sepulchres. What he needed was human warmth, the balsam of pity for the wounds he had suffered, comfort against the adversity which was silently hanging over him like an unavoidable spectre whose presence can be felt but not seen.

And just when his spirits were at this lowest ebb, a piece of news reached him which left him utterly confused and perturbed...

XII

Footloose

When Father Llàtzer received the bad news, he felt as though the black mountain-sides that walled him in had come crashing down upon him. Some women had arrived from the houses beyond the Ocata ridge to inform him of what was going on, and at first he could not make out what was on their minds or what they were talking about.

'A woman called Footloose?' he asked, quite bemused. 'But... who is she, this Footloose?'

Those women knew only too well. Footloose was the incitement to mortal sin: the local prostitute... She was the trollop of the woodlands, who, ranging here and there through valleys and over hillsides, had men old and young running after her, drawn by the enticing smell of fleshly delights. She attracted even some of the most decrepit old men, and even also some sickly youths, who used to come over all queasy at the thought of her... Whenever she turned up at a village or a hamlet, the women round about would be scandalised and say, 'Don't you know? Footloose has arrived at such-and-such a

119

place!' just like people say: 'In such-and-such a place they've got the outbreak, the plague...' When she was young and frisky she had rarely moved away from the lowlands, because in those days she had it very easy. She could blithely go from one town or village to another, strutting her fine, eye-catching skirts and brightly coloured headscarves. But later, when she lost her following in those places because she was getting wrinkled and the authorities were charging her with indecent behaviour, then she had no alternative but to go up to the hills or go down into a secluded valley, slinking into the woods or hiding in remote gullies, or finding a bolt-hole for a few nights in the strawloft of a local tavern or, on other nights, sleeping out in the open air. However, she had never yet set foot within the bounds of Montmany, perhaps because the terrain was too craggy and steep. That was why the women from Ocata could not come to terms with the idea that Footloose had appeared quite unexpectedly right up there at Puiggraciós. But this was not the strangest thing about the whole occurrence: because what most outraged the poor women, and what most disturbed Father Llàtzer, was that the people in charge of the sanctuary church had put up the harlot in their tavern.

'The shame of it! Oh Lord, the shame of it!' muttered the priest, deeply shocked to be told this. 'Who ever heard of such sacrilege? On church property, a place of worship, next door to the little sanctuary itself! Two steps away from the Mother of God, a whore like that, the damnation of men and the perdition of souls!'

Covering his face with his hands, as though shamed by the sins of others, the priest was pacing back and forth in long strides, until he finally said to the old man:

'Josep! Go up to Puiggraciós and tell the warden to come here at once... say I want to speak to him...'

An hour later Josep was back, head bowed, crestfallen.

'Up at the sanctuary, Father, they say they're very busy and they don't know how long it will be before they can come.'

The priest, although he was aware that this was just an excuse, waited until the following day. Then, when nobody came, he once again sent his man up to Puiggraciós.

'Go back up there again and tell them not to disobey me... One or other of them must come here immediately... Say that this is an order from me!'

When Josep returned he said that only the innkeeper's wife had been in, and that she had told him her husband was ill in bed and she couldn't leave him there on his own...

The priest had to struggle very hard to calm the turmoil of indignation raging inside him.

'Then go there for the last time,' he exclaimed, 'go in my name and give them the order to send that whore away, with no excuses or backtracking... to put an end to the disgraceful scandal they are creating!'

Back up the steep hillside he returned, and once more back down he came... The message that the old man bore when he appeared again was most disheartening: he said they had told him that they had no idea why on earth they should send the poor woman away from their hostel... she was not upsetting anybody... she was doing nothing wrong!

The priest was dumbfounded on hearing that reply. The disobedience of that couple at Puiggraciós was the first sign of the storm that for some time he had felt was brewing around him. The phantom of ill feeling and rancour, previously lurking invisible and impalpable, was beginning to show its face. He now knew on which front hostilities would break out in that war against him which was being quietly and stealthily prepared for by the woodlanders. Open revolt had begun at Puiggraciós...

and when he realised that it was more aggressively defiant than he could have imagined, the priest felt a strange shudder run through his body. His fear was now that, despite his resolve to face up boldly to any assault from his glowering parishioners, he would no longer have the power, exercised by him so far, to impose obedience by threatening eternal torment. He realised that henceforth he would be unable to make them quake with his threats uttered from before the altar, or to terrify them with his stares of indignation, or to lead them towards submission through fear of divine wrath. Up to that point the force of evil had shown itself indecisively, remaining bottled up within the deadened spirit of the woodsmen; but now it was beginning to take on a form, to acquire life and colour. Face to face with the power of God, embodied in him, there now rose up the power of Hell, embodied in the wicked woman installed in the sanctuary. The dark ravines, which he had been determined to redeem either through piety or through intimidation, would be torn from then on between two dominions... the dominion of God, in the parish church... the dominion of the Devil, at Puiggraciós.

'But, Lord, what must I do,' the priest exclaimed in prayer, 'to vanquish the evil spirit and to free from the base bonds of the flesh those wretched people who cling like ticks to the earth and all its sinfulness?'

Meanwhile the woodlanders had begun to go out and pry along the paths and tracks leading to the sanctuary at Puiggraciós. They were careful to avoid each other, prowling around while pretending that nothing was really afoot. And, when they got close to the buildings, they hid among the pines or the bushes in order to have a good view of the place. What they were really after was a glimpse, however fleeting, of that Footloose woman. They had heard so much about her that they were now sorely eager to see her; and then, having seen her once, they became impatient to have another look, as though they could not clear from their minds the obsession with the whore.

The whole Montmany district was now affected by the same never-ending temptation. By day, in the loneliness of the shady woods, young men and old had nothing else on their minds. At night, in silent and dark-filled bedrooms, they all tossed and turned under the blankets, dreaming or fantasising about that woman. Not a moment's rest did they enjoy, as the exotic image of the harlot preyed on their minds: the red hair like burnished copper; the abundant flesh, as creamy-white as curds; the faintest blemishes on her pale skin, like flecks of gold. To them only witchcraft could explain the fact that neither sunshine nor the cold night air had tanned that face, that neck and those arms to the same sunburned colour as all their faces, necks and arms. But then everything was so out of the ordinary about that woman, that Jezebel!

Was it not also rather strange, with all the rough treatment she suffered and the age she was, that she was still a fine enough figure of a woman to drive shepherds and land workers crazy? But the fact was that she had a look in her eye, a way of laughing, a bearing, something about her that was diabolically enchanting, something that the country women just did not have! They were all so darkly weathered, and so ugly, so desiccated, that Footloose shone like the sun compared with them. Not even the youngest and the most presentable among them could wear tight-fitting dresses like she did, nor strut and wiggle their bodies in the way that she could. Nor did they wear on their heads, instead of a rough cowl, a neat little headscarf like the one that she wore, tied so tightly with a big knot that it showed from in front the full line of the parting in her hair, and from behind her strikingly coloured tresses.

What was not at all strange, however, was that the strumpet's creamy-white figure and red hair should have promenaded day and night in the stolid minds of the mountain dwellers. There was a faggot maker from the Ensulsida property who, when he was out among the pines and was sure that he could not be seen by any charcoal burner or woodsman, would sit down calmly under a tree and take his purse from his sash. There he would begin to count his money, in order to see whether he had enough to be able to go to the sanctuary tavern and proposition Footloose over a drink. Or it might be a shepherd who, coming with a start out of the lecherous dream that dogged him, would leave his flock in the charge of his lad and then, secretively taking with him a lamb or a kid intended as payment in kind for the whore, would set off in haste up the track to Puiggraciós.

It seemed as though they had all lost their reason and their senses, and their instinctive nous about basic things, and perhaps even their general health. Daydreaming, mute, ruminant, they spent their time brooding endlessly over the carnal impulses which were exciting them. They could spend hour after hour without saying a word, staring fixedly without focusing on anything, seemingly lost in thought, making a deep groan from time to time, as though in the throes of a fever. It was a sickness caused by erotic mania, temptation, mortal sin... Some would cross themselves to dispel the disturbing thoughts filled with images of nudity that danced wildly in their minds... others recited psalms, prayers and paternosters... but still their derangement prevailed over everything... They were helpless to resist it, unable to break the carnal obsession which gripped them like an iron ring, unable to shake off the evil force whose talons were dug into their souls and their bodies.

Dark Vales

As soon as the early shades of night fell over the steep hillsides, first one then another, many were those who made their way furtively towards Puiggraciós. They were wrapped from head to foot in their cloaks, so as not to be recognised, like a procession of damned souls. Almost at their destination, they circled about, lurking either round by the church or outside the hostel buildings, as though afraid to go any closer. The Footloose woman, who often stood looking out of the window, simply made fun of the peasants' embarrassment, and every time they passed by or turned and went past again, she put her hand over her mouth, scoffing at them and laughing wildly... Or she would start singing strange songs, songs from far, far away, which rang out sadly through the tree-clad slopes, amid the silence of the night:

> *Somebody knows who I am,*
> *And goes off to denounce me.*
> *A chain is put round my neck,*
> *Not gold like ones I had worn,*
> *Presents from my fine lovers*
> *To shine both night and day,*
> *But now of weighty iron,*
> *Iron like the handcuffs too.*

The cowhand or woodcutter who plucked up courage, daring to be the first to cross the yard, rushed into the tavern, embarrassed and confused. Once inside, confronted by the strumpet's laughter, they stood daunted and dumbstruck. They wanted to say something, but just became utterly tongue-tied. There were moments when they would gladly have melted out of sight, virtually incapable of knowing whether they would prefer to get out of that place or to stay there.

The more Footloose stroked them and flirted with them, the more tormented they felt and the greater was their anguish. It was as if their suffering was physical, as if they were being prodded with a sharp goad... A strange sort of deep disquiet soaked into them, a mixture of panic and shame, and they began either to shudder or to break out in sweat... They were no good at making merry, or at having boisterous fun, or at cracking jokes, not like that woman who had been born on the lowlands and had lived in town! They were no good at such things... damn and blast it... no good at anything like that... and they just felt very awkward... And it suddenly seemed that, because of their embarrassment, all the fantasies about erotic pleasures, forged for themselves deep down in the woods, were almost vanishing into thin air now that they were standing face to face with the whore herself. They had gone up to the tavern to enjoy themselves and have a good time, but they had forgotten that they were dead souls... and the dead cannot enjoy a good time. The evil spirit of carnality had revived them momentarily... but all of a sudden they had been plunged back again into the habitual state of torpor to which they were condemned. Well might the innkeepers bring out food and drink for people spending the night under their roof; madam Footloose could get as carried away as she liked in her flirtatious play; but neither the wine, nor the good food, nor all the sweet talk, nor the fun and games could do anything at all to arouse gladness in the shrivelled hearts of the woodlanders. For them debauchery was a silent and sullen experience, with no excitement and no laughter, without enjoyment or cries of delight, like a good time that a gathering of corpses might have had...

When the first light of dawn appeared, the men who had spent all night at the inn headed homewards, feeling weary and faint, as though a great emptiness was in their hearts. But what was odd was that, as they went down towards their homes in the dark ravines, the image of the harlot appeared to them once more. The further they descended from Puiggraciós, the more they were revisited by the desire to see her again, the more the burning need was ignited to glimpse once again those visions of naked flesh, and the more they were all affected by that infectious pathetic sensuality which hovered like a feverous stench above the grim places where they lived...

Book-plate by Alexandre de Riquer, 1903.
(Biblioteca de Catalunya)

XIII

God and the Devil

In all of this the wretched priest was drinking deep draughts of bitterness. A taste of gall and vinegar lingered within him whenever news reached him of the peasants' debauchery. He would often weep, sobbing his heart out, as though it was he alone who had to be purged of the sins of each and every one of his parishioners… as though he alone, innocent as he was, must feel deep down all the pain of contrition that should have been felt by the numskulls of those hillsides, dragged down like dumb little brutes into the filthy ways of the flesh.

But at times he managed to hold back the tears welling up in his eyes, because he felt that they were not perhaps pure enough. He now and then felt a kind of remorse about shedding tears on his own account, especially when he had the vague thought that he was weeping over the rout of his private dreams of being a redeemer, rather than on account of the shortcomings and the sins of others. His heartfelt sobbing was cut short by the suspicion that such a human weakness could be the cause of his affliction, as the thought came to him that what was needed now was neither faintness of heart nor unmanly sighs nor childish tears, but courage, strength, to struggle against that bedevilled generation and to fell them with threats of an afterlife of eternal torment. The only important thing was to conquer the evil spirit of lust which had taken over the bodies of the woodlanders… Wailing, snivelling and weeping were not the way to vanquish and humiliate the powers of Hell.

'Strength of heart!' he said to himself, 'great strength of heart is what I need to overthrow the enemies of the soul! The raging threats of an irate prophet, words of execration, apocalyptic judgements are what I must hurl in the faces of my gnarled parishioners in order to wrench them from the clutches of the evil spirit!'

He was beginning to recall ancient ritual methods for driving out demons, and dreadful incantations for exorcism; terrible terms of anathema came into his mind as did the idea of barring the culprits from his church… While his head was being filled with such thoughts, he was all of a sudden taken by a different view of things, pondering that this might be just the time for a final act of piety, to make one last effort to achieve their redemption… This idea of formal indulgence gave him some hope, and so he sent his man once again up to Puiggraciós with the offer of forgiveness for the innkeeper and his wife, as well as for the strumpet, if they would come and confess their sins, and if they made a sincere declaration of repentance. But the reply which came back from the sanctuary church was that, as they had done nothing wrong, nor committed any theft nor murdered anybody, they had no need to repent.

Whereupon Father Llàtzer, deeply pained, understood that he was left with no alternative other than threats, imprecation, angry sermonising, promises of temporal punishment for the time being and eternal damnation in the future. He would have to do again what he had already done before... to wait for Sunday to come, to wait for the hour to say Mass. And then, when his peasant congregation were all gathered together and kneeling as he stood facing the altar... then would be the time to assert himself angrily and to impose obedience... Robed in the alb and his cassock, attended by all the sacred ornaments that had the power to make his parishioners bow their heads, he would be standing there, as God's justice-dispensing minister... He would wait until after the introit... after the epistle and the gospel... after the credo... and then, as soon as the time for the offertory arrived, he would suddenly turn to face his surly flock and begin to preach at them in a voice to make them shudder. He would first of all put them to shame by asking them one by one if they had been to see the harlot... They tried so hard not to be seen or recognised when they made their visits (as though God did not see and recognise everything!)... and he was going to make them blush with shame by forcing them to confess their sins in front of the whole congregation... 'You there,' he would shout, 'big lad from Ensulsida! How many times have you gone into the inn at Puiggraciós? And what about you, Cal Janet's next in line? And even you, Cosme, master at Rovira? And Bepus from Uià?' That is how he was going to single them out and disgrace them one by one, heaping embarrassment on them all in front of their own parents, their own wives and children.

Then he would set about challenging the guilty ones and reminding them that all their names were written down in the book of everlasting punishment. To have them erased, they must spend a whole lifetime in reform and contrition. Otherwise they would all be damned, and he could foretell for them from then, on every kind of calamity and wretchedness... the fury of the lightning bolt, enfeebling disease, the croak of starvation, the stench of fever... and then death, the death of the body... followed by another kind of death, much more terrible: eternal death, death in the flames of Hell...

The following Sunday, when the hour of High Mass struck, the priest had a face like thunder, terrifying to behold. His brow, usually so serene, seemed blotched by a frown which was dark like storm clouds; his lips, usually so kindly, looked pregnant with expressions of malediction and exorcism. Leaving the sacristy to go up to the altar he came face to face with his parishioners, and then his eyes blazed horrifyingly. The sympathetic and loving personality he always displayed now seemed to have been shockingly transformed, as though distorted by rage.

Old Josep, in his usual role of serving at Mass, rang the small bell, *ding-ding, ding...* and the office began. Straight away the peasants all knelt. Heads bowed and trembling, they dared not even look at the priest, fearing that he would turn round suddenly and with a single gaze would leave them petrified. So, when the introit was over and he turned to say *'The Lord be with you'*, all of them looked quickly at the ground so as not to meet the priest's scorching glare. What terror he inspired as he read the epistle, looking askance at them from close by the altar! Now he did not have at all the appearance of being a minister of divine grace, humble, loving, benign, anointed with the blood of Christ... Rather did he look like a preacher from ages past, about to prophesy both the destruction of a race steeped in sin and the fire from Heaven that would consume the land of the impure. The congregation recognised that the storm of holy rage was about to burst, and they shuddered every now and then with dread as if they knew that Heaven had been sorely offended and was going to hurl upon them every kind of malediction from on high. The moment was drawing closer, ever closer... The epistle was nearly finished... Then there would be the gospel reading... and then the creed... until it was time for the offertory as preliminary to consecration... and then... it did not bear thinking about... then the priest would turn to face them... Looking first to the right and then to the left, he would begin to pronounce sentence on them all, mixing taunts with rebukes, like the terrible Judge of Judgement Day itself... What anguish they felt! What anguish! Some of the men were quivering with fear. Others were using the back of a hand to wipe away the cold sweat of trepidation that glistened on their brows... The moment was drawing closer, ever closer...

But just when the woodlanders were feeling the sharpest pangs of their distress, as they saw that old Josep was about to turn the missal towards the participants... all of a sudden, in the enveloping silence of the Mass, an unexpected noise was heard: the brisk, gay swish of a skirt being whirled, like the sound that might have been made by a woman coming into church deliberately swaying her body from side to side. Everyone quickly turned to look; old and young felt their hearts miss a beat.

'God almighty! It's Footloose!' muttered the stupefied parishioners.

Yes: it was the harlot who was coming into the church having grinned at daft Bepus from Uià, at Cosme from Rovira and at the young master from Cal Janet who were nearest to the door, half kneeling, half seated. Then she passed between the rows of pews, her many-coloured skirt flouncing as she moved along and with a tiny scarf on her head, so tiny and daintily tied, that it revealed from the front the neat parting in her hair and, from behind, her blazing red tresses. Up the aisle she went, more than half way towards the altar, where she squatted quite provocatively, half gaping and half smiling. The parishioners, as if unable to get over the shock they felt, looked more dead than alive; and rising to their feet as the Mass book was turned in their direction, they exchanged looks among themselves, in a mood hovering between curiosity and fright, as if to say: 'What will happen now? What can come next? What will become of us all?'

Meanwhile, the priest, completely unaware of what was occurring, was beginning to read from the gospel, standing at one side of the altar, with that same severe look on his face, slightly bending over the missal. Then he stood up straight and he returned to the centre of the altar, to start to recite the creed. He began in a very quiet voice, almost whispering; but as he went through his recitation of the holy words, his voice rose gradually until he reached the sentence which says: *'He sitteth on the right hand of God the father Almighty; from thence he shall come to judge the quick and the dead.'* By this point he was almost shouting in rage, as though he himself was the tremendous Majesty who holds the keys of Heaven and of Hell...

But, lo and behold, something very strange had come over the woodlanders... they were no longer trembling at all. Up to that point their hearts had been squeezed tight, shrunken by fear... now, without knowing why or how, they felt them beginning to swell again. The priest could turn round suddenly to face them, and he could, as and when he wanted to, start sermonising them on divine wrath, because they now had nothing to fear nor any reason to feel cowed. Quite the opposite! Quite the opposite! They felt rather as though a huge weight had been lifted from them, and there were even those who gave a sigh of relief as they looked at the prostitute with warmth and gratitude, as though in her presence they found protection against the threats directed at them from the altar. The parishioners realised that the taunts and the damning threats would now be aimed not towards them but towards the loose woman, as soon as the priest saw that she was there. The impending clash would no longer be between them, glum and defenceless clodpoles, and the priest, dressed up in his holy vestments, armed with divine might. From then on he would have to confront the whore from Puiggraciós, that self-confident woman, so free and easy, who he himself said was the embodiment of the evil spirit. 'But is she really the evil spirit?' the peasants wondered grimly, without reaching an answer. They could not be at all sure about this, because their image of the Devil had come to them, among the shadows of night, only as the horned ram or the black cat, never had they contemplated it in the figure of a woman. But thinking about it now, this was what she must be because she so alarmed the priest. And now, right now the whole mystery was going to be cleared up... If that woman was indeed the spirit of Evil, who better than her to free them from the tyranny of the priest? For too long they had been enslaved by him, by that priest who used the Mass, the chalice, the paten and the holy ornaments to make them tremble and to impose his will as though he were the Almighty himself. All that was now finished, because the harlot, the spirit of Evil, would be their defence, and their salvation...

The parishioners were sunk in all these corrosive thoughts, when the priest, severe and haughty as though he were the statue of that God who had been insulted, turned to face the people in order to begin his sermon.

'Oh, you miserable people!' he began shouting, 'You hapless

ones, who cannot bring yourselves to fall on your knees before the Lord of Heaven and yet can worship the beast! When it is time to do the right and proper thing, you look dumbstruck and lifeless; but you stir quickly enough and come back to life in order to go and pay obeisance to the Devil, to go and slobber kisses on female flesh, to say prayers to God's enemies...'

But before he had even finished saying these words, he suddenly caught sight of the trollop and, pointing a finger at her, he broke the thread of his harangue and asked in a voice like thunder:

'Who is she, tell me, who is that woman over there who dares to come bareheaded into church? Who is that woman who comes to Mass with her head uncovered thus? Is she the one they call Footloose? Is she the harlot? Is she the wicked slut of Puiggraciós? Tell me! Tell me now!'

A funereal silence reigned everywhere within the church. No one dared breathe; no one dared look up. But what the peasants kept to themselves was made plain by the action of the whore when, rising from her squatting position, she stretched herself up to her full height with a provocative air as though saying: 'That is me.' And then there was a skip of delight in the dark heart of every one of the woodlanders, because they thought the moment of delivery had arrived. They all seemed to be joining forces with the evil spirit, urging it to bring down the priest and to lay him in the ground. But he stood firm, with an air that was haughtier, sterner and more majestic than ever.

'So,' he continued, 'so you are the woman of doom who replied with sneers and untruths when I called you to repent? So you are the woman in mortal sin who brings sickness to men's bodies wherever you go, and who extinguishes their souls for ever? So you are the Devil? So you are the way of the flesh?'

At each question the harlot stiffened, standing there straight and tall, with her body thrust forward and her head high, as though to defy and challenge the priest. It was a posture which could have been of feigned derision or a threat to claw the celebrant with her poisonous, fiendish fingernails: the very enactment of Evil incarnate confronting the might of God. There was a moment when she seemed to be on the point of taking a step towards the presbytery... But at that point the priest let forth a bloodcurdling roar, a noise like the sky being torn asunder. His eyes were flashing violently with the glare of an apocalyptic storm, and he raised his right arm high in the air as though to send forth the unerring thunderbolt of divine justice. He was the exorcist and the excommunicator... he was the priest wishing to drive infernal enemies from the bodies and the souls of the people.

'In the name of God the Father,' he shouted at the harlot in what was almost a howl, 'in the name of God the Father, who created the world out of nothingness... in the name of God the Son who gave his own life to save us all... in the name of God the Holy Spirit, who turned the darkness into light... I command you, evil spirit, to leave the church!'

The whore, who had turned a waxen yellow colour, suddenly staggered, as though her head were reeling, injured by the priest's incantation. She now looked like a cornered wild animal, with nowhere to turn, nowhere to flee to... In that instant of mortal anguish she turned her eyes towards the men she had been with in the sanctuary tavern, as though pleading for the smallest show of defence. She fixed her gaze on Bepus from Uià, but daft Joe looked the other way. She looked at Cosme from Rovira, and he just lowered his head. She threw a desperate glance in the direction of the young master of Cal

Janet, and the young master pretended not to notice.

Then the trollop, as though there were no firm ground under her feet, began to stagger back down the church, in retreat... but, before she reached the door, the priest bellowed at her:

'Repent! There is still time!'

But she merely turned her head to let out a devilish shriek of laughter: *hee-ya, hee-ya!* and then she went out, leaving the whole congregation dumbfounded.

XIV

White Mass and Black Mass

It was the Sunday after the whore had been driven from the temple under a hail of imprecations and anathemas. The tremendous words of excommunication, still echoing within the church, seemed to have stunned poor old Josep, who was there just inside the door, huddled up and somewhat confused, in the chilly darkness of the early morning. Grasping the rope which hung down from an opening beneath the choristers' gallery, he rang the big bell unhurriedly to call people to Mass: *Dong... dong... dong...* The more he rang, the more faltering and indecisive the peal sounded, just as if those already trembling hands pulling on the rope had lost the knack of getting a steady rhythm... *Didong... didong... dong.*

Each strike of the bell struggled to carry through the gorges and under the cliff faces of the district, as though it dared not climb the slopes to call as usual at the doors of slumbering houses, with its regular Sabbath song: *Come, neighbour... the Mass to hear... come neighbour, come!* The mist that morning was so thick, so thick and so cold... it really seemed as though the chilly dampness that floated all around had frozen the bell's voice.

The old man, although he was generally so long-suffering, every now and then had to let go of the rope in order to rub his hands which were turning numb. 'A fine start to the winter!' he muttered. 'The Lord could send us a better start to the winter!' And to bring the feeling back into his feet, which were also quickly becoming numb, he shuffled a few painful steps, now inside the nave, then out into the porch and back to his position under the gallery. And then, once he felt a little better, he began pulling the rope again with as much enthusiasm as he could muster, pausing occasionally to make sure he could hear the peals. But he was becoming so senile and so hard of hearing that he could not be certain whether the bell was ringing out or not. 'God on the cross help me! Perhaps I'm not making any sound,' he grumbled gloomily.

And in fact, although he had been at his bell ringing for a good long time, not one man or woman had yet turned up for Mass. 'Perhaps I'm not doing it properly, and the people can't hear the sound of the bell,' old Josep started muttering again. Eventually, in order to find out the truth, he headed outside to ask Mariagna, because she, although weighed down with woes and afflictions, was not as hard of hearing as he was.

'Can't the bell be heard, Mariagna?'

'I can hear it well enough, Josep.'

'So then… why are they not coming?'

'Oh, it's certainly time that they were here!'

And the old couple looked at one another, bemused, unable to fathom what was happening.

Meanwhile the priest, standing by the escritoire in the sacristy, was donning his vestments for the celebration of Mass. As it was so misty and so dim at that early hour, it had been necessary to light the stub of candle standing on a candle holder, to make it possible for him to see anything as he was robing. The day was one of those when dawn never arrives, the kind of day that begins in grim darkness, like another night coming directly after the preceding one. Through the little slit window which gave a view of the apse there came not a glimmer of light from the sombre sky outside. Everything was gloomily overcast. However, in spite of the depressing emanation that seeped everywhere, Father Llàtzer felt uplifted that morning by the most powerful faith, and on his lips there even flickered a kind of triumphant smile.

Memory of the victory he had obtained the week before, his triumph over the demon of carnality, filled his heart with confidence in his power as a priest anointed by the agency and grace of the Almighty. He felt that the spirit of God was residing within him, since he had shown sufficient spiritual strength to confound the enemies of the soul. Never before had he understood so well that, adorned in the holy vestments, he was performing the office of Divine Majesty, with the three crowns of Glory upon his head, with the blazing sword in one hand and the chains in the other to subdue and fetter the forces of Hell.

As he passed the alb over his head, he reflected that his terrifying outburst had been powerful enough to bring down the harlot, to bring down his parishioners, and... why should he not confess it... to terrify himself by unleashing those dreadful words of exorcism. The horror which he had felt then had been so overpowering that he had been unable to find the strength of heart to preach at the woodlanders and to draw out from his moral victory the whole stream of lessons and examples that the situation had presented him with.

But what he had failed to do the previous Sunday, disturbed by a mysterious dread which sprang from the execrations he himself had proclaimed, he would now do forthwith, as soon as the time for the offertory arrived.

'So you can now see, brothers and sisters,' he would say to them, 'you can now see how victory belongs always to God, to the Lord of the Heavens and of Earth who has only to lift a finger in order to return this world into nothingness! If you follow the way of the Lord, you will be going arm in arm with the Saints, who triumph eternally. If you go along the path of sin, your own feet will lead you into disaster and death. The pleasures of the flesh last for only the blinking of an eye, and God's joy endures for endless centuries. In the flesh is where sickness and damnation lie dormant; health and eternal life throb with the spirit of God. Come with me, those of you who wish to live for ever! I shall show you the way of the light that is never extinguished... I shall let you see the tree of life, whose leaves never fall...'

'Father!' exclaimed at that point a half muffled voice as of someone who dared not interrupt the priest's exaltation.

Father Llàtzer turned round, and he saw the old man approaching with a wan look on his face, a look that was truly pitiable.

'What is wrong, Josep?' the priest asked in a kindly voice, on seeing the dismay of his poor old helper.

'Dear me, Father! I just do not know. I do my best to make the bell ring out... but nobody wants to come.'

'Has no one arrived for Mass yet?'

'Nobody at all, Father, nobody.'

And as though to reinforce what her husband had just said, behind him appeared Mariagna shaking her head in a show of despondency.

The priest stared at the old couple for a good while, filled with surprise and alarm, more because of their look of desolation than because of the sad words they muttered. Never so much as then, never before, had he seen them looking so downcast and at the same time so pained. The two of them, who were never usually unsettled by anything at all, now seemed to be consumed with anxiety.

'Don't you see that because it's such a bleak morning... they must be waiting until the last moment,' the priest said benignly, in order to raise their hopes. 'Start ringing the bell again for a short while... will you? And then you can sound the final fast peal... God does not want us to jump too quickly to negative conclusions, nor to despair about what might be in store for us.'

As humbly as could be, old Josep began tugging again on the rope with all the eagerness he could summon: *Dong... dong... dong...* Meanwhile his wife was going back and forth, all restless: into the church she went and then out she came again, peering now towards Uià, now towards Rovira, impatiently looking out for people to appear from the woods. But the combination of the weather, which was very overcast, and her own poor eyesight meant that, however hard she looked up and down the paths leading there, she had not a glimpse of a single human being, not a living soul... until finally, at last, below the narrow terraces of Cal Pugna she thought she could make out a troop of people approaching from that direction. It looked like a shapeless patch in the landscape, some parts of it white and other parts black, which stirred and moved along, going forward through the trees, although it was impossible to recognise clearly what it was.

In order to be sure, the old woman went to have a word

about it with Josep… and peering from beneath the hands which they had each of them stretched over their brows, they stood looking towards the cliff face, both of them straining to see if they could make any sense of that strange phenomenon.

'There are people coming… Don't you think so, Josep?'

'It looks more like a flock of sheep to me, Mariagna.'

'A flock of sheep? Do you really think so?'

'That's what I reckon it is…'

And, while the old couple were doing their best to dispel the painful uncertainty they each felt, the wriggling patch they were looking at disappeared all of a sudden, as if swallowed up behind a ledge on the cliff, leaving no way at all of telling whether what they had seen were woodlanders or sheep. At this point Josep and Mariagna finally lost patience. Although usually so submissive and staid, that Sunday they both looked really perturbed and worried, just as if they were afraid that something dark and nasty was about to happen. Like souls in torment they went back and forth from the sacristy into the church, from the church out to the cemetery, from the cemetery to the paths leading there…

'They're getting old, poor things… doddery and confused,' Father Làtzer kept saying under his breath.

But eventually the agitated behaviour of the old couple began to make him feel anxious. Accustomed as he was to seeing them so steady in their ways, taking everything so calmly, he could not come to terms with how jittery they now were. But what was most distressing and painful for the priest was when he realised that he himself was being affected by the restlessness of his servants.

'And what if my flock weren't to come down here to Mass?' he now was thinking somewhat alarmed. 'What if they were to give up on the church for ever? If they no longer wanted Mass or sacraments any more?'

A quarter of an hour went by, half an hour, and then a whole hour... and still no sign of life. The priest, fully decked out in his robes and still standing his ground by the escritoire, finally grasped the chalice and then went out resolutely to the altar. As he stepped into the presbytery, he could not refrain from glancing into the nave to see whether the odd parishioner had turned up: but with so many shadows heavily thronging the building, he could make nothing out at all clearly. Only the deathly silence which reigned there disclosed that not a single living being was drawing breath in the place.

The day itself, instead of becoming brighter, was turning more and more overcast and gloomy. Neither the tiny glimmer of frosty brightness that leaked in through the church windows nor the trembling flicker of the candles on the altar were enough to dispel the darkness that spread everywhere. Only the stronger light that came from the tapers on the credence table was sufficient to project a kind of luminous haze onto both sides of the tabernacle, while the two candle holders placed below the statue of Saint Paul barely managed to bring a slight shine to the sword of the stocky apostle. Everything else was shrouded in a thick limbo-like gloom...

His heart overflowing with grief, Father Llàtzer was groping by the altar as he put down the chalice and shuffled the pages of the missal which he had taken out of its pouch. The irremediable sadness of that day of gloom was dripping into his soul, as though intent on drowning it in overwhelming darkness. 'All alone!' he sobbed. 'I have been left all alone.' And such was his distress in this tribulation that he could not keep his mind on the ceremonies he must perform nor on remembering the words of the Mass. The most he could do was to try to retain some serenity and lift his spirit towards God… but at each step he took in this painful effort he felt a new stab and another nail driven into his flesh.

The first time that he turned towards the church door in order to say *'The Lord be with you'*, it seemed as though his heart was being torn asunder as he saw that the greeting of love was echoing in nothingness… *'The Lord be with you…'* and yet the pews were empty, all of them empty… 'But where are you, oh my wretched parishioners?' the priest asked through clenched teeth. 'Where can you be, you fugitives from the blessing of Heaven?' And then, as though it were a mysterious response to his question, he suddenly heard a distant voice which revealed to him the place of damnation in which the woodlanders were at that moment gathering.

What had happened was that, instead of setting out as usual towards the church, the men of the parish had headed uphill to the high ground at Puiggraciós. The womenfolk were as keen as ever to go down into the hollow where the church stood in order to attend Mass, following the command uttered by the bell… but the men had stopped them from setting foot there. 'Don't go down there, do you hear?' they said to the women, staring hard at them. 'If you want Mass, go to Sant Segimon, or go to Ametlla, or to Bertí, or to Figueró… but whatever you do, stay away from the parish church…'

And then, willy-nilly, the white hoods had set out into the mist on their different ways to the neighbouring places of worship. The men meanwhile, wrapped in their capes, were climbing the steep slopes up towards Puiggraciós.

With what appalling clarity was everything now making sense to the priest! At that very point in time, with the White Mass about to begin down in the ravine, where there was just emptiness on every side, the Black Mass was beginning up at the sanctuary, with a considerable throng in attendance…

As though he were blessed with the gift of being able to see distant and hidden things, to the eyes of the priest, as he stood now by the altar table, there appeared quite vividly the bizarre spectacle being enacted inside the building up the hill. He could see the smoke-stained rooms of the tavern filled with people and brightness… and to him they seemed like the nave and the presbytery of that temple of sin where worship of the Devil was being performed. The main fireplace, with flames from bundles of twigs blazing and crackling loudly, looked to his eyes like the high altar of Hell itself, adorned with burning logs and their flames which cast a sinister light upon the dark walls and upon the weather-beaten faces of the peasants. He could make out a vision of a figure like that of a locally venerated saint, there in front of the blazing altar, which was the presence of the spirit of Evil, embodied in the harlot. There, lounging on the fireside settle, Footloose dominated the scene as though occupying a triumphal throne, showing off her vivid red tresses and the starkly white flesh of her neck, her arms and the swell of her breasts. Around her circled anxiously, like worshippers afraid to go up to the altar, the young master from Cal Janet, the lad from Ensulsida and daft Joe from Uià, all those gloomy young men, drained of strength by lecherous thoughts and a deep sadness…

Mortified by that sacrilegious apparition, the priest kept closing his eyes in order not to see it. But the ghastly awareness of events in the sanctuary stayed with him, perfidiously pursuing him throughout his celebration of the Mass. When he came to the consecration, he imagined again who was officiating at the Black Mass being celebrated at Puiggraciós. They were the innkeeper and his wife, that old couple, now appearing partly like sorcerers and partly like those roving songsters who would intone a psalm for a small donation. Coming and going among the tables in the tavern, they were serving food and drink to those present or taking messages to the whore on behalf of farmhands, wood cutters or shepherds. It was as though they were priests in Hell's service whose duty it was to convey to the Devil the litanies that were inspired by mortal sin.

Father Llàtzer felt that he was moving towards the brink of emotional breakdown, as though he were about to die. When he came to recite the final prayers, he could barely utter a single word nor hold himself upright before the altar. Then he turned round, as usual, to give the dismissal; but, as he was about to pronounce the sacred words 'You may leave now: *ite missa est*,' he suddenly hesitated, refraining from voicing that expression which seemed to chime in with the sacrilegious insult being directed at him by the woodlanders. Instead, he moved directly to the final gospel reading, speaking with a tremulous voice, and then he picked up the chalice in order to return to the presbytery. But he was so pained and affected by such turmoil, having struggled so hard to get through to the end of the holy office, that he felt his legs give way beneath him as he went down the two steps from the altar. His head was spinning, and after stumbling for an instant, he collapsed to the floor as though mortally wounded.

The chalice flew in one direction, the altar linen in another, and the paten hit the ground even further away... Old Josep and Mariagna rushed to his assistance: 'Father! Father!' But the church was in such darkness that they could not see where to put their feet in order not to trample on the priest. And also... on the ground where they stepped lay scattered the parts of the sacred service of Mass, and they were terrified to think that their profane hands might touch the chalice cup or the contents of the altar linen, or even the inside of the paten… But, finally overcoming their terrified religious scruples, they moved towards where the priest had fallen, stretching out their arms in the darkness, and they felt the fabric of his chasuble…

'Father! Father!' they exclaimed.

'Father!' they repeated, 'Father!'

But the priest showed no sign of regaining consciousness.

Sanctuary church and watch tower at Puiggraciós, 1950.
(Salvador Llobet/the Municipal Archive, Granollers)

XV

Dark Days

Winter had set in relentlessly, with its constant succession of short days, faded sunlight, lowering skies and slack drizzle.

Winter is a sad time everywhere, but nowhere on earth more so than there in those dark vales, always inhospitable and sunk in shade. On days when a cloud trailed a long black patch across that sky hemmed in by the encircling hillsides and summits, the inhabitants might well declare *'God help us'*, because darkness lingered eternally in those ravines, as though it felt snugly at home there... In all the hours of endless, dispiriting gloom people in their houses had to grope their way around. Neither wick lamps nor lanterns gave enough light for the women to go easily about their housework, cleaning and airing the bedchambers, going up into attics or down into cellars.

Some days it seemed as if the already deep ravines had finally sunk down into the very bowels of the earth, and that the woodsmen were living now inside the dense nothingness of limbo.

But even worse was when, on top of the depressing darkness, there came the days of never-ending rain. Sometimes it was a persistent drizzle, treacherous even if not violent, of the sort which, without making any noise, turns field edges into sludge and soaks into every wall, saturating the ground as far down as it can reach. At other times it was a ferocious downpour which swelled to their limit all the cascades and filled every watercourse with a rushing torrent. It seemed that the flood would sweep away everything in its path. And as if it were not satisfied with inundating vegetable gardens and cultivated terraces, it tore stones out of field walls and banking while turning the tracks into flowing streams.

What groaning and cries of anguish could be heard then! What weeping and complaining in the time-worn houses! With the tracks all boggy, with water standing in the fields and the ground ravaged, people were besieged in their homes and threatened with starvation. They needed to eat... yet they could not go outside nor get to their vegetable patches to gather food. They ran out of bread... but they could not go down to the flour mill.

'It's all because of that evil wench,' the women said. 'It's because of that trollop up at Puiggraciós: that's why God is punishing us so!'

'The parish church and its curses,' muttered the menfolk, 'are what have brought about these dire troubles!'

And as the downpours went on endlessly, rain upon unceasing rain... even more tribulations and tragedies were caused. The water exposed the crumbling foundations of houses, or it produced rot in the ends of structural beams, overflowing from the guttering on all sides of the buildings. One day there would be shouts of 'Come here, quickly!' because roof tiles over a stockyard were crashing down...

152

Then it was 'Get a move on, make haste!' as water rushed between buildings and poured into cellars... Scared to the very core of their being, people hurried to prop up ceilings which were quaking on the point of collapse, or to pack holes and cracks in walls with handfuls of straw, with old rags.

'Our time is up!' shouted terrified women.

And the men responded in hoarse voices:

'God blast us if we can't all die here and now, so we could have an end to our suffering!'

But, pray as they might or curse as they might... the water was not held back either by oaths or by paternosters. Down it came, incessant driving rain, sometimes in torrential downpours, as though the end of the world was nigh... at other times in a persistent gentle drizzle, as if tired by its own efforts to drench everything, it was no longer in any hurry and could continue to fall until Judgement Day. So that winter the rain-filled hours dragged by and dark days followed dark days... until one morning, above the terraces at Uià, the sun began to show its face very hesitantly. But what a sickly and feeble sun it was! It seemed incredible that broad daylight could show such a poorly face and watch the world with such a deathbed countenance!

The ravines were very soon tinged with a faint shine that was ashen and yellowy, itself evoking thoughts of death...

Old Josep and Mariagna also drank the daily cup of sorrow throughout that period of dejectedness and gloom. All alone and abandoned in their troubles, with no consolation or support from anybody, there were times when they would gladly have commended their spirits to God's love.

Senile and doddering though they were, the two poor souls had still been forced to defend themselves against the treacherous water which even came in through the roof tiles and through gaps around windows and doors. So as not to be caught unawares by the enemy, they scurried about like ferrets, keeping an eye on doors, windows and openings in the building, and they took turns to keep watch day and night in order not to fall asleep through exhaustion. While Mariagna was on watch, the old man would take a nap: and when they came together at the change of shift, 'May the crucified Lord help us,' he would groan, and she would reply, 'May He help us for ever, amen!' Those prayers were the old couple's way of greeting one another, providing mutual support in their distress and their solitude.

Among all the travails they were enduring, what made them most confused and anxious were the leaks, which as time went by, were pouring ever more persistently from all the ceilings. How their nerves were tormented by this! There is nothing on earth as disturbing as hearing in the dark the sound of dripping water: *tock, tock...*

On some nights the old woman, overcome with fatigue, would flop onto the bed only to feel, before she had even closed her eyes, drops of water falling on her head. 'God, my Lord, help me!' poor Mariagna would shout as she was moving to get up. And then there she was, going towards the landing with the lamp in her hand, stopping suddenly in the doorway because she thought she could hear drops falling also inside the adjoining closet. That was where their meagre clothes were kept, so she rushed to take them out of the trunk, fearing that they would get damp and mildewed. Hanging the oil lamp from a peg, she began to gather together her precious garments... But as soon as she had picked up all the clothing, ready to move it to a safer place, she realised that rain was also coming into the storehouse outside... and as that was where the year's barely sufficient supply of grain was kept, she simply did not know which way to turn or what to salvage first. It was unbearable… a desperation comparable to staring death in the face!

Some days later, when the bad weather lifted slightly, it did seem that the old couple ought also to show signs of pulling through… But this did not happen. For one thing, that pallid sun depressed them deeply… and, moreover, they were continually beset by fresh difficulties and new things to torment them. When it was not calamities caused by the weather, there were other troubles and matters to worry about. Poor things! The older they became, the more their character was changing. Whereas previously they were never unsettled by anything at all, they were now becoming crotchety and fussy, as if they were being gnawed inside by their worries. From the way in which they were losing their grip and becoming ever more fretful, complaining and whimpering all day long, they seemed like souls condemned because nobody prayed for them.

They were forever moaning that the water had made a mess of everything but that they were no longer capable of repairing all the damage. And so they came and went at all hours of the day like agitated goblins, murmuring mysterious worried words into one another's ear.

Josep would say, under his breath:

'What will he say when he sees all of this?'

And the old woman would reply pensively:

'Oh dear me! What will he say?'

Cowed and bemused, they both looked outside and saw that the waters had swept their vegetable plot down into the rushing stream close by, that the paths were now lined with a fresh growth of wild grasses, and that the crosses in the cemetery were lying among the mallow plants, no longer upright because of the downpour and the wind. But most alarming of all was when they went back inside the church for the first time and saw the destruction which had been wreaked there. Water had got in under the door, leaving the stone paving covered in thick sludge; the clothing on the statuary had become infested again with mildew, and spiders once more spun their webs along the altar cornices. What pangs of self-reproach beset the old couple as they contemplated all that filth! They felt guilty and also ashamed for being so old and so powerless to prevent the devastation.

And so they kept crying out:

'What will his reverence say when he sees all this untidy mess? What will he say when he sets eyes on this?'

And when the priest did come down from his room, grim-faced, sallow, much older-looking, as though years and years had been piled upon him, the couple seemed to want to hide, as if they wished they could melt into the ground.

Bedridden for weeks with fever and delirium, it was to the spectacle of drab skies and grim weather that Father Llàtzer finally opened his eyes and looked once more upon life. How desolate, how sad, how utterly forsaken did everything appear to him, now as before!

In the sinister light of that wan and dingy sun, the circle of dark mountains which walled in his existence had never before seemed to him so funereal. Rather than being born again into the light of day, he felt that what he was doing was merely changing his place of entombment. Thus, just as until then he had been buried deep in his sickbed, henceforth his grave would once more be the blackness of the ravines. His return to the bizarre existence of a man who has been buried alive seemed to him to be the most frightful punishment and, at the ` same time, the awful sign that he had still not served the full term of the sentence delivered on him by divine judgement. He had imagined the good fortune of never having to see again that forbidding landscape of cliffs and deep gorges nor those patches of thick shade beneath the wooded slopes... He had been dreaming of never having again to hear anything about those sluggish people who hatch wickedness under the cover of sleep and who, enticed by the demon of carnal pleasure, abandon the Mass and the holy sacraments... He had glimpsed the light of the bright star announcing the end of his personal Calvary... He had felt almost cleansed of his previous short-lived transgression and had been looking forward to enjoying celestial forgiveness... And now he was once more a prisoner of darkness, chained to the foot of those cliffs and of those towering mountain sides!

In order to soften somewhat the chastisement of coming back to the life to which he had been condemned, he could find no other consolation than to think back over everything that had come into his dreams during those hours of fever when it seemed that he had already passed over into the next world. With his eyes closed and his head held high, like someone savouring in their mind a pleasing vision... he took such great delight in contemplating again the funereal spectres which had danced for him at the foot of his bed among all the mists of his delirium!

First of all he recalled a great darkness, a deep blackness, like that which the dead must see in the burial places where they repose. But then, all of a sudden, against that background world of nothingness, some tiny sparks of light began to flash, making the dark seem even denser. They were shimmering little lights, moving in all directions, disappearing and then reappearing, skipping here and there before his eyes... 'Wait a moment! This means that I am dead,' he thought, 'dead and buried... and these tiny lights must be the will-o'-the-wisp which flits through the cemetery.' But the idea was immediately checked: 'No: that is quite impossible: if I was lying in a grave I would not feel, as I can do now, that rain is falling on me...' And there was no doubt at all in his mind that he was being rained upon... 'I could have counted one by one all the drops falling on my head. But how to explain that those little lights kept coming and coming, as though wanting to draw close enough to touch me? So close were they that I finally saw they were not the will-o'-the-wisp. They were wick lamps, the ones carried by Josep and Mariagna when they came to attend to my needs. At first I could not really understand what they were doing when they were moving the bedclothes and turning over the counterpane; but later it became clear to me that what they were trying to do was to grasp the edges of the sheet and between them move me to another place... What I could not work out was if they were taking me out of that room in order to find me shelter from the water that was dripping onto me, or else... if my final hour had indeed come and I had to be buried, were the old man and woman each holding one end of the shroud to carry me to a hole in the ground? It was something which never became clear to me, never...'

In this way, seated inside the entrance to his house, Father Llàtzer called up memories of the disturbed state of mind he had suffered while he was ill, as though trying now to stitch together mentally snatches of dreams and layers of wild hallucination... And then, suddenly he seemed to be awakened from his visions of the grave and to focus on the here and now. In a faltering, trembling voice which betrayed a weakened spirit, he called to the old couple:

'Josep, Mariagna, come here, please! I need to get some

fresh air. Help me to stand up... we are going outside... I want to see the church, and my garden...'

Upon hearing these words both of them seemed to freeze inwardly. The old man looked at his wife, as though exclaiming silently, 'It is the moment that we so feared!' And his wife shook her head, as if to say: 'Oh dear, what shall we do? What will he say when he sees all the damage that has been done?'

One of them walked on each side of the priest, supporting him, and as they went along the couple were thinking, deeply worried: 'Any moment now, he is going to see what has happened and cry out in anguish.'

The fact is that what made them both fearful was not the thought of being rebuked by Father Llàtzer, but rather the prospect of hearing the quietly pained laments he would utter so often, more hurtful than any reprimand.

Once the priest was outside and he had raised his face towards the circle of hills and cliffs surrounding him on all sides, a taste of bile and vinegar surged up within him as he had never experienced it before, not even in the times of his greatest, most grievous suffering.

The sickly pallor of the sunlight gave the landscape a quivering, tearful lustre, gelatinous and funereal, and the ravines seemed like the realm of eternal stillness on the last day of the earth. A sepulchral silence floated all around and struck a chill into the heart. Frost stiffened any rustling of leaves in the coppices, ice held back the flow of water in the ditches. No breath of life could be heard, no sound of animals, no whisper of a breeze... Everything was silent, as though life had stopped, as though everything in heaven and on earth was about to disappear for all time. Even the impoverished, dilapidated houses scattered here and there on the lower slopes looked as though they were suffering, as if they were seriously ill, even perhaps about to die. At Uià, the winds had bent the chimney on the single-storey kitchen and had knocked down the turret on the oil press, so that the farm as a whole seemed to be lopsided. At Cal Pere Mestre the rush of the water had burst through the stretch of wall between the gateway and the stockyard; and the big gaping hole made the building look as if it were opening wide its mouth in the final throes of death. Can Pugna, its external walls now propped up with beams and big timbers, was like a house with a serious limp, so crippled that it needed crutches. The unstable walls around Romaní, which had been sagging ominously for years, had crumbled away even more, so that they were now teetering precariously over the steep slope below.

Father Llàtzer placed his hands in front of his eyes in order not to see such desolation.

'This is death!' he said to himself. 'This is death which is surrounding me on every side, pulling faces at me, coming close as though to touch me but never laying a hand on me! The fields are dying, the houses are dying... everything is dying except for me. And how, in my despair, I yearn for eternal peace... The houses will surely collapse in ruins... Without shelter, there will come a time when the peasants here will have to seek refuge in caves while they await the final hour... Then all of this will be turned into an immense graveyard, an unbounded cemetery... while I... I shall still be alive, as though designated by God to watch over the sleep of the dead...'

But the priest's black thoughts were suddenly cut short when, as he looked down at the ground, he was surprised and horror-struck at the sight of the garden. Seeing how ravaged was that patch of land, previously so full of abundant plant growth and now completely razed... he seemed to be on the point of heaving a great sigh to give vent to his dismay. The old couple's heads were already bowed as though they felt in advance the embarrassment they would be caused by the woeful expression they were about to hear. But the priest, in order to spare his servants from such distress, choked back his lament and managed to keep it to himself, merely directing a pained look at that now lifeless site which he had once regenerated through his love.

Then he took a few steps further, directly towards the church. As soon as he reached the cypresses in the cemetery he was heartbroken to see, along the path edges, weeds growing again, in greater lushness and pomp than ever. 'He will not be able to avoid moaning now...' thought his aged companions apprehensively. But the priest, silent still, moved forward with his eyes closed, as if not wishing to see the depressing dereliction surrounding him.

At last they came to the church itself. They pushed open the door, and they were confronted at once by the desolation which reigned in the holy place... blotches of mould on the garments of the saints' statues, cobwebs draped along the cornices and in the niches of the altars, a carpet of slime all over the floor, debris and rubble everywhere... At this point the priest's anguish exploded in a single outburst, while the old couple felt a cold sweat, a sense of deep unease that made them all of a tremble...

'Enough, oh Lord!' shouted Father Llàtzer. 'I can bear it no longer! Do not punish me any more, for I declare that I submit to your infinite power!'

Then he turned to Josep and Mariagna, and pointing at the calamitous condition of the whole church interior, he asked them in a tone of profound sadness:

'But what is this? Tell me! What is all this?'

The old couple, though, instead of replying began to whimper, with tears running down their faces.

'Are you crying?' the priest asked the old man.

'I am crying,' was the reply.

'But, why? Tell me why...'

'Because my strength has gone, Father.'

'And you, Mariagna, Mariagna!'

'Because we are both useless.'

'Oh! You poor things! Do not ever talk like that: you are tearing my soul to shreds!'

And, as though poleaxed, quite defeated, with his head sunk in his hands and with an intensely disquieting feeling under his skin, the priest reflected that the deathly loneliness of which he had earlier dreamed a vision was nothing like as cruel as the solitude which he now knew was in store for him. He was about to be abandoned by his aged companions: their strength was at an end and they could die at any time... And he, all alone, helpless, would be left to wander without direction, like a drifting phantom, in that valley of the shadow of death.

XVI

Howls in the Night

Father Llàtzer was quite unable to soothe the sharp pain that he felt in his heart from being shunned by his churlish parishioners. How could those perverse people have turned their backs on the church? To think that they had rejected their own place of worship and its pastor! To think that they had spurned the Mass and the sacraments! Not in his brief conversations with the old couple, nor in the long hours of his daily prayers, nor when he stood before the holy altar, never could he rid himself of the sinister memory of the woodlanders and he was constantly tortured by it.

'What a sacrilegious insult!' he said to himself. 'What cruel taunting!'

Obsessed with these thoughts, he spent hours turning them over and over while in his mind's eye he saw the shadow of the harlot or that of the tavern keepers at Puiggraciós, of the pathetic, lecherous young men who turned the sanctuary into a brothel, or of the decrepit old men of the ravines, spiritually hideous and physically cankered. At times he even felt a kind of shame that his own spirit, having once been endowed with wings on which to soar up to the shining summits of divine contemplation, was now brought down to the level of an insect or worm, incapable of raising its head out of the dirt on the ground. What anguish he suffered, in his lowest moments, when he felt that his soul was now chained to brooding cogitation of this kind!

'Having failed to redeem the rude and untameable people of the hills,' the priest mused bitterly, 'all that is left to me is to stay trapped in the meanness of spirit that pervades this harsh land! Oh, Lord! My feelings are of rancour when I am yearning to feel pity and kindness! Instead of anger about everything around me, I wish I could feel love!'

But, no matter how much he urged his spirit, he was unable to be rid of the acrid taste of the bile which overflowed in his breast. He wished he could be like that loving father who, the more he is disappointed and let down by his son, the more sacrifices he makes for that same son. But he felt that his own heart was not generous enough to take charity to such lengths... The old wounds which he bore, instead of healing over, were festering more and more because of the frequent affronts and taunts insidiously aimed at him by his furtive parishioners.

And those people of the sad woodlands spared no effort to goad him, pricking his running sores and prolonging his suffering. There was indeed scarcely any malicious ruse they would not resort to, in the dead of night, for the sake of cruelly mocking the priest and his aged servants. Sometimes, after dusk had fallen, they sent a youth to climb up the church tower, take the clapper from the bell and hide it, so that Josep would not be able to call people to Mass the next day. On another night they would dig a hole in the middle of one of the paths near to the priest's house, covering it over with greenery and brushwood, to see if any of the three people there would be caught unawares and fall into it. Or similarly under the cover of darkness, they would go out to divert the water from the pool which irrigated the osier beds, directing it straight towards the house so that their vegetable garden was flooded and they could not gather food for the kitchen.

Each of those evil deeds was another sharp sword driven painfully into Father Llàtzer's heart. And it was not the evil act itself which most tortured the priest, but rather the blind hatred that lay behind it. He himself was such an unworldly and benign individual, and yet he was confronted with the blackest treachery! Love was the dominant instinct in him, but he had come up against the fiercest of hatred!

'What harm have I done to them?' he sometimes exclaimed. 'What harm have I done to them, unless it was to offer them life anew, trying to cure them of the ravages of sin?'

At other times he pondered that there might still be a remedy if he were to make one final sacrifice, one last effort. What was needed, he thought, was for him to take himself up to Puiggraciós at a time when they would all be gathered there to make merry. He would arrive and face up to the farm workers and shepherds, the charcoal burners and the wood cutters; he would confront the innkeepers themselves, and the Footloose woman herself... And there he would preach to them with the greatest fervour, until he had softened their hearts, until he had touched the most tender part of their souls, until he had reduced them to tears... It would be the occasion when, he imagined, he would manage to produce that outpouring of sweet words which he had previously never succeeded in finding... 'My brethren, my dear brothers,' he would say to them, 'I am here to bring you salvation, even though you might not want it. I feel pity towards you because you, without knowing it, have been innocently blind since birth... But I have come to open your eyes to the splendours of the heavens and of all things on earth... I pity you because your hearts are shrunken and withered; but I will open your hearts to gladness and to brotherly love.'

But then he had second thoughts and said to himself: 'No! It is not for me to go in search of them... I am the shepherd of that flock, God's anointed one... My appointment is by Divine Majesty... It is they who must come to do penance... It is for them to bow their heads so low that they are covered in dirt...' But no sooner had his thoughts gone in this direction than his mind was changed again as he recalled the acts of humility performed by Christ in order to bring men to forgiveness and to peace. 'Was it not He,' he protested, 'who stepped forward to confront sinners in order to remove the stains of their guilt? Was it not he who gave himself up to his tormentors who would torture him and then lead him to be sacrificed?'

In this endless weaving and unpicking of his doubts, so spiritually enervating and physically exhausting, Father Llàtzer's whole life was draining away...

The truth is that the same obsession which tormented him by day also kept him wide awake in his bed at night. His head was filled with the restless, nagging phantoms, the remnants of his earlier delirium, and so every night he watched in the darkness the silent procession of the night hours. In the vast stillness that surrounded him, he had become accustomed to distinguishing the faintest, most feeble sounds... and so he spent long hours listening, listening in the dark, as though he were trying to decipher the unknown language of the thousands of beings and things which speak or sigh, which yelp or weep meekly in the great silence of the night.

The rustling of dry leaves disturbed by tiny creatures on the ground; the stirring of the tree tops when the branches suddenly feel a puff of wind; the gentle trickling sound coming from an irrigation ditch; distant noises made by sheep and cows moving now and then out in the fields; the muffled cry of the invalid turning over in the bed where their life is coming to its close... these were the sounds which combined to form deep in the ravines the chorus of the night, mournful and disturbing, like a murmur coming from the other world. Father Llàtzer's ears were attuned now to identifying in the dead of night the different calls of the fearsome nocturnal birds which nest in the cracks of cliff faces or in overhanging branches above a chasm. He could recognise the terrifying drawn-out screech of the eagle owl, and he knew the nightjar from its grating cry of complaint. His efforts to penetrate the abysses of silence brought on feverish hallucinations and strange states of exaltation: at times he seemed to hear sobs which came from nowhere and mysterious echoing noises, resounding inside his very being, like the moaning of a soul in torment. At other times it was as though the sound he heard was coming down from the high pass at Puiggraciós, a sound which rang in his ear like a diabolical peal of laughter and made him shudder with indignation.

'They are having a party at the sanctuary...' he muttered in great anger. 'They are having a party, making fun of me, mocking me just like they mock the Mass and the sacraments... It is the same devilish laughter which rang out in the church when the excommunication was pronounced.'

And then he immediately envisaged, as though he were witnessing it directly, the performance that was being staged probably at that very time in the sanctuary tavern. He could see the strumpet, seated on the bench by the fire, trying to excite with her enticing laughter – *hee! hee-hee!* – the pathetic lasciviousness of the torpid peasants. And, welcomed by the innkeeper or his wife, in wandered the clients: shepherds and labourers, charcoal burners and wood cutters, cowherds and pigmen. One by one they all shuffled inside, like birds with ruffled feathers, looking awkward and with their eyes to the floor. And they all walked past where the whore was sitting, as though paying tribute. It was a silent and glum procession, like a queue of corpses. At its head was the young master from Cal Janet, gazing downwards as if making a solemn vow; a few paces behind him followed the Margaridó lad, as unapproachable as a wild boar; and then Cosme from the Rovira farm, his face jaundiced and his air downcast; behind them came daft Bepus, from Uià, with his red hair and nasty look… And after these four, in traipsed all the other young men from the hillsides and ravines, a troop of youths and lads, all showing the same combination of embarrassment and surliness…

But the parade of pathetically lecherous figures did not end there, because following along behind, with their capes held up to conceal their faces, one after another came the heads of households and doddery old gaffers, all of them outlandish in appearance or physically impaired. There was Pau Malaric, as gaunt as a mummy; old man Sunyer, with his flabby cheeks and watery eyes, more like an ox than a person; the old buffer from Lledonell, uncannily resembling an owl with his round face, startled eyes and tiny nose; Pere Mestre, with his faltering limp that made him hop like a frog; grandfather Pugna, whose heavy goitre and head covered in lumps gave him a toadish countenance… The postures of these ugly creatures were either stooping or aslant, and they all moved along grim-faced as though going to a burial service... There were only two people at that funereal party whose faces showed any sign of enjoyment. One of them was Aleix the truffle man who, twisted and coiled like a snake, was alone in a corner, with a sneer on his face that seemed to express disdain for that train of lascivious cadavers. The other was pumpkin-faced Carbassot, the swineherd, whose wisecracks and crazy pranks provided entertainment for all the denizens of the dark ravines. That night he had hit on the idea of chanting some lines he had made up in order to amuse the strumpet. He was wearing clogs and before they knew it he was beating out the rhythm of his ditty by banging his feet on the tiled floor:

'Clip, clop, clippety-clop
Clippety-clippety, clop, clop, clop!
The priest is out of his job;
No more preaching from his gob,
As all his parishioners
Went off to Puiggraciós.
Clip, clop,
Clippety-clop
Clippety-clippety, clop, clop, clop!'

And sure enough, the whore broke into a mad cackle of laughter, *hee-hee! hee-hee!* until she could keep it up no longer... It was so often at this point that Father Llàtzer would wake up from those nightmares that persistently beset him like a charge of alarming apparitions.

One evening, after finishing his prayers, with the breviary still in his hands, he went into a kind of daydream as he contemplated from the window of his room the strange patches of cold light that the moon was spreading over the landscape outside. With his head pressed against the glass panes, peering at the hazy images of the winter's night, it was as though he was trying to hold at bay the awakening that he must soon experience.

There were moments when he was thrilled to observe how the blue-tinged brightness gave an argent hue to the terraced fields and the low-lying patches of land, which looked to him just like silvery pools. At other moments he was fascinated to watch how the same effect of colour melted away, as if swallowed up in an abyss, as soon as it fell upon the thickness of the woods and upon stretches of ground that were overgrown with vegetation… But it sometimes happened that the fantastic light show could be obliterated, when it was blotted out by black clouds coursing through the sky like a flight of crows. The priest was captivated, bewitched, by those mysterious effects of the moonlit night, with all its dreamlike manifestations, shifting between the dominance of darkness or of brightness. It was as if in a dream that his half-open eyes espied the dark patches formed against the marmoreal whiteness of the paths by the black crosses in the graveyard. Lifting his gaze slightly, he could then discern the jagged outline of pinnacles that were traced on the church walls by the slender tops of the cypress trees.

Father Llàtzer's state of mind had been in a constant fevered turmoil of dreams and brooding anxieties ever since his recent illness. But at this very moment he felt that he was held suspended in ecstasy before the obscure, mysterious spiritual presence of the night… This trance he was in became steadily more overwhelming, and it was as if he must surrender totally to the hypnotic, spellbinding power that was influencing him… But then, quite suddenly, he raised his head and with a kind of start was brought back to his senses…

A dog had howled: a low, bass howl that resonated through the cliffs and across the hillsides like an agonised groan, *ahwoooo!* It was one of those eerie cries which produce a shudder in the person who hears it in the dark and alone, for it is a sound which betokens long death throes and croaking last gasps... *Ahwoooo!* How that poor animal was crying out! How it was moaning! And oh what pity was aroused by that desolate call as it faded away into the peace and quiet of the mountains, into the dappled nightscape! The priest, now suddenly all of a shudder, strained to hear from which direction came that lugubrious portent of a person's final spasms.

'It seems to be coming from the other side of the cliff...' Father Làtzer began to think, with some uncertainty, when he heard the distant barks of other dogs responding to the sinister howling. 'No.' he then declared, correcting himself. 'From the other side of the Can Ripeta col, now I think the sound is coming from there... But, wait, that's not it...' he changed his mind immediately, 'the yelping is coming from Puiggraciós.'

Indeed it was from up there that the disturbing noise made by the dogs first came, echoing down the steep hill to where he was. The initial soul-chilling howl could now scarcely be heard, as though it had been dispelled in the immensity of the night... but as that pained yawl faded, the yelping of the other dogs was redoubled, in a racket that resounded ever more loudly, as if quickly coming nearer and nearer. The first dogs to join in the barking seemed to be the ones at the sanctuary; those at Can Coll joined in next; then the ones at Rovira; by the end, even the dogs down the hill at Uià played their part in amplifying the din.

At this point Father Llàtzer looked up with eyes which seemed illuminated with some vague brilliance, as though a scintilla of hope had shot through his being. What all that clamour clearly meant was that somebody from up on the ridge was coming down towards the church. And, as if in his heart some slumbering hopes were suddenly being raised, without his clearly understanding how or why, he began to think that the person approaching was some helpless parishioner coming in search of succour from his priest, coming to implore divine forgiveness, to solder anew the chain of love which had been broken through sinfulness.

The noise made by the dogs sounded closer and closer. The barking of the ones at Rovira was coming now from the pond below that farmstead, so it seemed they had accompanied the traveller as far as the slope down to the osier beds.

'He cannot be far away now...' Father Llàtzer muttered to himself, looking out of the window.

It was not long until a rustling was heard coming from the direction of his vegetable garden, a rhythmical sound of footsteps that rang out in the stillness.

'Here he comes...' murmured the priest, bringing his head up close to the window panes. 'Here he is...'

A moment later, the figure passed through a patch of light and could momentarily be picked out clearly, so that the priest could see the person who was making his way hurriedly towards his house: one-two, one-two... Whoever it was looked to be a young man, determined and fearless. He knew where he was going and he made his way without hesitation, like somebody quite familiar with the route and able to follow it in the dark. Once he had passed by the vegetable garden, he crossed to the other side of the path, cut through the row of cypresses, went into the cemetery, passed in front of the church and then made a sharp turn to approach the house. There was silence for a moment... The person must have been groping to find the door knocker. Then it was in his hand: *Bang, bang...*

XVII

The Road to Calvary

When old Josep heard the knocking on the door, at that late hour of the night, he rose from his bed as quickly as he was able, despite all his infirmities. And, putting on some clothes as he limped along, he made his way towards the entrance. There was a mixture of suspicion and fear in his mind because he was constantly aware of the woodlanders' dark schemes. But in fact, he was much relieved when he heard, coming from the other side of the door, civil words spoken by the man who had come to disturb his slumber.

'Who is there?' asked the old man.

'Somebody who comes in peace,' the stranger replied.

'Say who you are…'

'I'm the shepherd from Lledonell, up at Puiggraciós.'

'And what were you wanting?'

'I've been sent because the old lady at the house is at death's door and is asking for the last rites before she passes away.'

'Then I'll go and tell his reverence…'

'Please do, and God bless… and meanwhile I shall go

quickly to Figueró to ask the doctor to come at once… although I fear it might be too late…'

And with these words on his lips, the man set off down the hillside, very soon becoming lost from sight among the shadows of the night.

Old Josep meanwhile was going up to Father Llàtzer's bedroom to give him the news, but he encountered him already at the head of the stairs. The priest's face was brightened with a kind of celestial smile and he said:

'I heard everything. We must go up there… Come on. Saddle the mare at once… If you cannot do it alone, get Mariagna to help you, or if not I'll come myself…'

The old man, with all his usual patience and humility, went off to do as he was bidden, without fully understanding that look of fervent gladness which lit up the priest's face.

'Ah, perhaps tonight I shall be able to make peace with my parishioners!' Father Llàtzer said quietly to himself as he opened his house door to go out to the church.

'Up there, at Lledonell…' he was thinking, 'I shall find the people from round about all gathered at the sick woman's bedside… I shall speak such words that will move them, that will touch their hearts, if God aids me with his grace…'

As he was about to go through the cemetery, a sudden gust of freezing wind made him shudder. It was a bitterly cold night, overcast… the air was damp… the sky in mourning clothes of pitch darkness, without a single star. The clouds, which a moment ago had been flying like crows across the face of the moon, had now covered it completely with their wings of blackness…

The priest opened the church door and went inside, heading for the presbytery. There he crossed himself and knelt; then he stepped up to the altar, where he first gave a bow, and then immediately another one, lower still. This done, he moved to one side the main tablet inscribed with the words of the office, being able thus to open the tabernacle and reveal the sacraments... Then he made a genuflection that was lower even than his previous ones, and as he raised himself up with his hands on the edge of the altar, he was thinking of the words of divine love he would speak to the dying woman at Lledonell, promising her the glory of God, offering her an eternity in paradise... and all of this would be performed to be heard by the neighbours who would be attending the Communion, so that they, reawakened, should experience a new revelation of the divine promises... Then he took out the sacramental bread and placed it with great unction in the pyx, his lips moving gently all the time in fervent prayer. Finally he hung the cord of the small casket round his neck, and he walked back down the church, back the way he had approached the altar, but now majestically, filled with ecstasy, as though transfigured by the glory of being the bearer of the consecrated Body of Christ himself.

At the door he found the old man waiting for him, bell in hand, standing by the mare fitted with saddle and trappings. Also there was Mariagna who was lighting the lantern that would guide their steps through the darkness.

Clang, clang! Clang, clang! Josep rang the bell excitedly, as though desperate to announce to the world that no less a highness than God himself was deigning to leave his palace in order to visit a dying sinner. The priest meanwhile mounted the mare, and then he intoned quietly the resonant line from the psalms:

'Have mercy on me, oh God, according to your great compassion!'

Clang, clang! Clang, clang! responded the old man,

wielding the bell with all his might to make it ring out loud and clear, while his wife covered his shoulders with a rug to protect him against the damp coldness of the night.

Then the two men set off on their journey. Mariagna, kneeling outside the church, watched as they left her behind by first going through the cemetery to cross the row of cypresses, then turning off the pathway. The old man went in front with something of a limp and taking each step carefully, because, encumbered with the bell and the lantern, he had difficulty in leading the mare by the halter. On his mount the priest came behind, with head bowed and his hands crossed upon his chest, as though embracing the Holy Sacrament he was carrying. Only occasionally did he look up and then begin to chant in a low voice, as though praying, another plaintive versicle:

'Wash me, wash me thoroughly, Lord, from my iniquity and cleanse me from my sin!'

Clang, clang! Clang, clang! was once again the old man's response, as if the sound of the bell was the right accompaniment to the holy words of the priest.

But both the words from the psalms and the sound of the response merged into one, like a cry of pain, unheard by any living creature, lost in the immense darkness. The night was so cold and so misty it seemed as if the damp chill that seeped into everything was freezing the chant of the priest and the resounding note of Josep's bell. But this did not make either of them desist: the chanting of the one and the ringing of the other continued amid the silence and the solitude, as though they were the grateful bearers of the most exalted, mysterious message. Onwards, steadily onwards, they followed the edges of the small fields at the bottom of the tight valley. The tracks there run along flat ground and rapid progress can be made.

Sometimes limping, sometimes not, the old man got his head down and pressed on, with the lantern and the bell in one hand and holding the mare's halter in the other. Behind him came the priest and his mount, onwards, steadily onwards...

But just as poor old Josep was on the point of striking up the gentle slope towards the osier beds, he was dismayed to find that his legs suddenly felt weak. With the rivulets that continually ran down the bank from the pond, the ground there was always damp and slippery; but now frozen hard, it was even more treacherous to walk on. The old man stumbled frequently, and the mare had to keep stopping for a while before setting off again on the climb. In the dense darkness all around, and along that track which was now so narrow and steep, the journey up was becoming more and more wearing and dangerous. With just the flickering light from the lantern, the old man did not have enough aid to see where he was putting his feet; and because he was stumbling all the time, he began to feel terrified of falling into the steep gorge which lay to one side of the track uphill. And so he kept on praying, under his breath as he went:

'God protect us from harm!'

When, after a while, they reached the oak wood on the slope below Rovira, because they were getting closer to places of habitation, the priest sang out the sacred chants in a louder voice:

'Behold, I was shapen in iniquity; and in sin did my mother conceive...' he voiced with sombre feeling.

And as though wishing to harmonise with the rising solemnity of the liturgical chant, the old man prepared himself to ring the bell vigorously, as loud as he was able, and he let go of the halter by which he was leading the mare. This freed his right hand to take hold of the bell, but then he suddenly felt the ground give way beneath his feet... Although the priest quickly reached out a hand to steady his man as he staggered, it was too late, and in vain... Josep, lantern and bell all went tumbling down the hillside, not coming to a stop until they hit the stream bed at the bottom of the gorge...

'God in heaven... help me!' cried the old man in a pitiful howl, while Father Llàtzer leapt from his mount in order to rush to his aid.

But everything was enveloped in impenetrable darkness, so that the priest had no idea how to negotiate the precipitous drop.

'Where are you?' he called, gripped inside by deep anxiety. 'Where are you, Josep? Tell me where you are!'

'Down... down here, your rev... reverence!' came back the faintest of voices from the depths of the gorge.

Guided by the old man's cries of distress, the priest made his way down, then he searched and searched until he found him. The priority now was to have some light on the scene, in order to see the extent of Josep's injuries; and, while Father Llàtzer was striking with his steel to get the lantern lit again, he spoke words of encouragement to the old fellow in that compassionate tone which so befitted his lips:

'Poor Josep! Brother of mine! Fear not, for God in heaven is with us!'

The old man could only whimper in place of a reply, as though his gasping prevented him from forming words. He was lying stretched out on the ground with his legs wide apart, beneath a knotty cluster of old roots which protruded, twisted and gnarled, from the steep clay bank. That was where he had landed and that was where he lay, as though he had been knocked out. His legs were giving him much pain, one foot was quite dead, his face and hands were covered in blood.

Only with much heaving and straining was the priest able to get him upright in order to start going back up the steep side of the gorge.

'Have courage, Josep! Be brave!' he kept telling him.

Mustering every bit of energy they could, they struggled together up to the track, close to where the mare had been left. But by this stage the old man had lost all his strength and coordination. At each step that he tried to take, his legs gave way beneath him. He tried to grasp the halter, but still he could not keep his balance. Then Father Llàtzer, as a last resort, attempted to take hold of the old man bodily and heave him up on to the back of the mare. But to his surprise, Josep stiffened in protest at this, refusing to be subjected to the manoeuvre, objecting vigorously with his head and his eyes: no, no!

The priest was taken aback by such unusual disobedience in a man who was always so resigned and so humble. That unexpected stubborn resistance was quite incomprehensible. But a moment later he understood the whole crisis. Josep's behaviour signified that he would never consent for the body of Christ to travel on foot while he, a poor sinner, rode on horseback. Even though he was moved by his servant's ardent piety, Father Llàtzer had no alternative but to make felt the full weight of his own will.

'I am giving you an order. Do you understand? I am ordering you to ride.'

On hearing this, the old man bowed his head, and the priest, putting every bit of his being into a supreme physical effort, heaved Josep up from the ground and managed to get him seated on the back of the mare, securing him as best he could in the packsaddle.

Hunters, c. 1920.
(Courtesy of the Municipal Archive, Figueró-Montmany)

XVIII

Sacrilege

And so the dolorous cavalcade continued on that road to Calvary. In front, the priest with the Holy Sacrament hung about his neck and resting on his chest; lantern in one hand, and halter in the other. Behind him, the poor old man, slumped sideways on the mare, like a wounded soldier.

Onwards and upwards, the priest was striding out confidently, following the winding path that led from the main track to the heights of Puiggraciós. Rather than subdued after the recent harsh setback, his mood was calm and determined, as though he had just prevailed in a confrontation with the spirit of Evil and was now savouring his victory. Onwards and upwards, it seemed that he was being guided by the heaven-sent promise that he could win round the woodlanders, vanquishing insults and treachery though love and charity. So valiant did he feel that he recalled unconsciously the lines of the psalm that proclaim the rewards of forgiveness and mercy: the words came to his lips and he intoned softly:

'Purge me with hyssop, and I shall be clean; wash me and I shall be whiter than snow.'

He was exalted and emboldened by the psalmist's vehemence, and in every one of these words he found a mysterious meaning that applied to his own trials and tribulations.

'Make me to hear joy and gladness; that the bones which thou hast broken may rejoice.'

Onwards and upwards, every so often he looked in the light of the lantern at the face of the old man drowsily slumped in the saddle. Or he resumed his singsong psalmody. And so the climb continued, ever upwards along the route made by the feet of generations past through the centuries-old pine woods... until a cold squall, much colder than the air he had been breathing until now, hit him full in the face...

He had reached the top of the ascent, and leaving now the shelter of the gorge, he was immediately exposed to the chill winds which blew at those heights. Up there, no longer held in by the imprisoning walls of cliffs and ravines, the wind came and went, rushed and swirled freely over the ridges, whisking away the hanging mists that rose up from the valleys. This was a cleaner, a purer space. Even the darkness here seemed to be less dense and less thickly packed than down below. And from here he could make out the shadowy shape of the sanctuary at Puiggraciós, the clay-daubed walls of the tavern and the seemingly whitewashed façade of the little church.

The priest could now breathe easily, with the satisfaction of the person who begins to see that his travails must soon be over. Just beyond the church were the old houses in a small cluster on the upper part of the ridge, and not far beyond them was the solitary farmstead of Lledonell, some way down the other flank of the hill, as if it had stepped across the watershed and was on the point of descending into the further valley. Father Llàtzer felt, on the one hand, urged on by his desire to redeem, to save souls; on the other hand, his spirit was gripped tight by the fear that he would never be able to make his peace with the woodlanders...

Passing in front of the inn, his heart missed a beat at the mere thought that the people inside might appear and that at any moment, he could be confronted by the Footloose woman and the couple who kept the place. But none of these fears materialised. The stillest silence reigned all around, and not a chink of light was visible anywhere in the building.

Then the priest, as though suddenly moved by remote inspiration, stopped in his tracks and halted the mare. Standing there, square on to the inn, he began chanting another verse from the penitential psalm:

'Then will I teach transgressors thy ways; and sinners shall be converted unto thee.'

The manner in which he pronounced these words, with such feeling and such fervour, made them sound like the very voice of contrition itself knocking on the door of the unrepentant sinner. But the only response to the mysterious admonishment was in the silence of the still night. No sound at all came from the tavern, the scenario of rustic debauchery, which stayed as quiet as the grave.

Father Llàtzer pressed on determinedly, thinking that nobody would be coming to meet him until he had reached the dwellings on the ridge. But, as soon as he came to the cluster of old houses, his spirits sank when he saw that there was not a sign or a shadow anywhere of the inhabitants.

'Perhaps the Lledonell people will be waiting in their yard...' he now mused, clutching at a straw.

But try as he might to sustain confidence in his sacred ministry, he could feel his spirit being increasingly overshadowed by the blackest suspicions. The closer he came to Lledonell, the more his mind was troubled... And chilling beads of cold sweat appeared on his brow when he espied the vague outline of the farm chimney against the dark backdrop of the sky. Then he thought that the turret on the building was coming into view, and next a shape which might have been an outside porch, and finally the bulk of the big farmhouse itself, with its yards, its sheds and its hayricks... But of people there was no sign at all... not a soul, not a single living person... Everything was shut up, locked and barred... Not a glimmer of light was coming from any window, nor from a doorway, nor from anywhere at all...

Father Llàtzer's heart was beating frantically, pounding as though it were trying to burst out of his breast. Even the old man, shattered though he was and awkwardly slumped on the packsaddle, kept raising his head and showing his own great anxiety. Upon reaching the threshing floor in front of the house, the priest let go of the halter, and, as if suddenly taking his courage in both hands, he went determinedly to knock on the door:

Bang! Bang!

A good while went by: nothing... there was no answer. Again the priest knocked:

Bang! Bang!

The same silence as before.

Bang! Bang! Again he hammered on the door, this time more loudly.

Then it seemed that a sound was coming from inside there. Steps could be heard, making the floor creak as they came towards the entrance. Finally a window was opened and a man put out his head:

'What do you want at this hour?'

'We have had word to come and give comfort to an old lady who is close to dying…'

'Where were you told it was?'

'Lledonell…'

'This is the place… but we don't have anybody here who is in a bad way.'

On hearing this, the priest staggered backwards, as though on the point of dropping senseless to the ground… but then, folding his arms across his chest, as if to embrace the holy objects he carried there, he ran in despair towards the old man:

'Josep, we have been deceived!'

Josep said not a word, but tears were streaming down his face…

'If you want to come inside to take some rest…' offered the man at the window, apparently feeling sorry for them.

'No,' was the priest's immediate response as he took hold of the halter on the mare and turned again to make the journey back down into the depths of the ravine.

Stay there? Not a moment longer, not even long enough to say a brief prayer… What he wanted was to be away from there in a flash, to disappear for ever from the infernal place he was in… What mockery, what cruel mockery from those evil-minded enemies. He could forgive the taunts they aimed at him, and he did forgive them wholeheartedly… but… to deride so the Holy Sacrament! To mock the Body of Christ! What greater sacrilege than this?

With such thoughts in his mind, his spirit tortured by them, the priest fled quickly, as quickly as his legs would carry him, tugging at the mare. As the starlight began to fade, he realised that it would soon be dawn, and he felt afraid, mortally afraid, of being up on that accursed mountainside in the light of day. When he went past the houses on the ridge, the people there would probably rush out to look at him, to scoff and to insult him. And the mere thought of this brought a burning discomfort to his cheeks, a scorching, excruciating blaze of embarrassment.

The vexation he felt was not on account of himself, a poor hapless priest, but of the Holy Sacrament that he was carrying on his person. That was why he was now rushing desperately back downhill, because he thought that to expose the Body of Christ to the taunts of those godless peasants was like exposing the Saviour, once more, to the affronts of the scourges and the thorns, the mockery of the purple robe and the sceptre of cane, the shame of death on the cross, the sponge soaked in sour wine and gall...

How insufferably heartbreaking it all was! As the route took them past the hamlet on the ridge, even though the priest was rushing as though driven by a storm wind, he thought he could hear doors and windows being opened and also muttered sounds everywhere of scoffing and mocking. But the most distressing thing was shortly after this, as he was about to cross the yard in front of Puiggraciós sanctuary... That was where the Footloose woman would perhaps be, together with the innkeeper and his wife, the shepherds, the charcoal burners and the wood cutters, all the people who had contrived the whole hellish deception...

In order to be safe from vicious looks and sacrilegious insults, the priest guided the mare slightly away from the main track, so that they could go by below the level of the yard without being seen, concealed by the banking. But, as soon as they went into the first pine trees of the downwards slope, Father Llàtzer heard a shriek of diabolical laughter that sent a devastating shiver through his whole being.

Hee, hee-hee! Hee, hee-hee! It was the same infernal

laughter that he used to hear coming from the sanctuary during the long sleepless nights after his crisis… the same shrill cackling which had resounded in the church that Sunday when he had pronounced the excommunication…

At this the priest abruptly quickened his pace, rushing down the hillside, driven by the urgent desire to deliver the Body of Christ into safety from the insults and the abuse proffered by those irredeemably damned inhabitants of the tree-clad ravines.

Wild boar hunters.
(Courtesy of Paquita Dosrius)

Sheep gathering, Gallicant, c. 1910.
(Courtesy of the Municipal Archive, Figueró-Montmany)

XIX

Death Throes

'Josep, come quickly, up here!' screeched Mariagna from the landing outside the priest's bedroom.

'Josep, come here, for the love of God!'

But, as neither hide nor hair of the old man appeared, his good wife could only make her way to the window looking onto the cemetery and from there start wailing again into thin air:

'Josep, for God's sake! Be quick, come here!'

She was looking out in great agitation, now in the direction of the vegetable patch, now towards the main path, now towards the line of cypresses. But her eyesight was failing badly and for the life of her Mariagna could nowhere see her husband. And so, growing more and more impatient, all she could do was to keep calling out in her cracked, thin voice:

'Josep, come! Do be quick, Josep!'

And the sad thing was that the old man was really quite close at hand. At that very time he was just coming under the cypress trees, heading towards the house. But he was so hard of hearing that he heard none of his wife's cries. And what is more, the poor old fellow had barely enough strength to put one foot in front of the other because of that painful limp of his. Ever since he went crashing down into the stream bed, the night they were going to give the last rites to the dying woman at Lledonell, he had not been himself. Now he moped around the whole day long, and every step he took was accompanied by his groaning complaint, as if he were muttering a roll call of all the saints: 'Lord, be by my side! God help me! Lord, have pity on me!'

That is why he did not hear a word of poor old Mariagna's pathetic calls as she was screaming herself hoarse from up at the window, until finally, exhausted and whimpering, she went downstairs intending to go outside to see if she could find her husband. The little old woman's movements reflected her anxiety and her desperation… as if driven by imminent calamity, she looked capable of forcing herself to cover as much ground as might be necessary… And then, as she reached the doorway, without having seen him, she bumped into Josep, who had come limping along in the opposite direction.

'Oh dear, Josep, come quickly, don't tarry so!'

'But… what is wrong? Bless me!'

'His reverence is in a bad state… He is on his way out!'

'Dying, do you mean? God help us!'

'Yes, dying… if he isn't dead already. I called him… and he did not respond; I called him again… and he still did not say a word; I touched his hand… and it felt as cold as ice…'

And with tears in their eyes and fear in their souls, the old couple went back inside, all aquiver. It was not the image of death which scared them, for they were well used to seeing it from close up, as well often having to feel it with their own hands… They knew only too well, from their duties as rural sextons, what it meant to keep watch over a corpse, to dress it for burial and to consign it to the grave... What terrified them was the thought of the horrific solitude that awaited them among those dark hillsides as soon as his reverence's eyes were closed for ever. Holding hands just like children, the two of them went together up the stairs, eager to be at Father Llàtzer's bedside, and nervous at the thought of the great mystery in which they were involved, the great mystery of a poor human soul departing for the next world...

The room was cold, bleak, bare. With the headboard pushed up against a wall, the bed stood a couple of feet above floor level, beneath the outstretched arms of a large crucifix. At the other side of the room were two big chairs and a small table with an oil lamp on it, and above this furniture, there was a shelf full of books and papers. There was nothing else to see except the whitewashed walls, with discoloured patches here and there caused by leaks in the past, stains which snaked down the wall from ceiling height.

The old couple went in with cautious steps, almost tiptoeing as though fearful of disturbing the sacred silence of a life which was now drawing to a close. No sound was to be heard, neither sighing, nor hoarse breathing nor panting... Filled with the respect that closeness to the mystery of death inspires, they moved slowly towards the bed, and in the flickering light of the lamp, they now peered to see if the moribund body there was still breathing at all.

'Father!' shouted the old man, his voice choking. 'Father!'

But the priest neither moved nor made any sound, lying there like a stone effigy.

Then the old man took hold of the hand that was resting on the bedcover, and when he moved it to his lips in order to kiss it he felt the frosty chill. As well as cold, moreover, it felt heavy, so heavy that, when he let it fall back on to the bed, it dropped there like a stone. Poor Josep felt his own spirits failing, but as though determined not to lose the last glimmer of hope, he wanted to make sure of the evidence before admitting the terrible certainty of the calamity that now befell them. In order to dispel their distressing doubt, to know for certain whether their master was dead or alive, he would have felt his chest, checked his heart and breathing, if the dying man had been a man like all the rest. But as if bound by a holy respect, he dared not place a hand on God's minister, on the one anointed in Christ. He went no further than to take the lamp and swing it gently in front of the priest's eyes, to see whether his pupils showed any response and followed the light. But there was only a glazed and fixed look.

At this the old man's head drooped, as if to say, 'There is nothing to be done,' and turning to his wife, he spoke to her in a solemn tone:

'Mariagna, his reverence is dead. Let us both kneel and pray for his soul.'

And, as the old couple fell to their knees at the bedside, each muttering the Lord's Prayer, the priest made a great effort to speak; but try as he might, he could say nothing... The truth was that Father Llàtzer was not dead, not yet... He could hear clearly what they were saying, he could make sense of everything going on around him... but he could neither turn over nor make any movement, and to speak or to give any sign of life was impossible for him. If only he had been able to shout out loud, he would have said to them: 'What are you going to do? What are you going to do? Stop your drivelling, you hapless things!' But since he was incapable of opening his mouth, he could not call their attention... and when the thought occurred that they might bury him before he was dead, he felt gripped inside by the blackest dread. 'This is the punishment for my shortcomings!' he thought in horror, while the couple were praying on their knees at his bedside. 'It is the punishment for my sins, to be buried alive! I was full of life when I was consigned to the black grave of these ravines... And I shall be alive, alive when they lay me to rest in the church graveyard. It is a sentence that has always hung over me, to be treated for ever and a day like a dead person! What an awful damnation for someone like me who has always sought the sunlight, who has always been a lover of life! I got caught up in a consuming fancy to bring back to life a thinker of centuries long past, poking into and digging about in the grave which were his books, declaring that all the world's truth was to be found there, and I tried to make a saint out of a heretic. And becoming more and more arrogant in this mission, I pursued it relentlessly until I fell into the pit of sin, the death of the soul... Then came my punishment, to be exiled to these ravines shrouded in shadows and steeped in sadness... and even here, even in this land of unconsciousness and of death, I attempted to bring forth the gush of dynamic action and of life. I wanted to resuscitate the lifeless woodlanders who stalk the dark tree-clad slopes with the appearance of having a life and a soul. But instead of my inspiring them with the life force, it is they who have given the kiss of death to me... In the effort to open their eyes to the eternal light, I have submitted to mockery, to being deceived, to being spat upon, to being physically and spiritually martyred... and now, as my reward for all this, they will be helping to bury me while I am still alive and breathing, and they will even come to dance upon my grave...'

While these awful apprehensions were drifting like ghastly shadows in and out of Father Llàtzer's consciousness, the old couple, having finished their funerary prayers, stood upright making the sign of the cross upon their brows, on their eyes and on their mouths. And then the old man said to his wife, very deliberately, in that low voice which people use in the presence of a dead body:

'Mariagna, stay here, close by, to watch over his body… and light at each corner of the bed those four snuffed candles there on the shelf…'

'And you, Josep, where are you going?' she asked very respectfully.

'Me, I am going to the church… to ring the death knell for his reverence.'

'May God keep him in holy glory!'

'Amen,' replied the old man, adding later with a note of mysterious unction: 'Then, when I come back here… we'll prepare to put him in his shroud.'

As Josep was limping out of the room, horrified thoughts ran through the priest's mind: 'Woe is me! If only I could say something! If only I were able to give a sign, to get through to them! How to stop them from making the bells ring out, sounding the death knell? When the peasants hear it, perhaps they will come down here, to come in and see me, perhaps then to put me in the ground while I still live and breathe, hastening to throw earth on top of me in order to finish once and for all their evil work!'

These thoughts were quickly followed by a procession of disturbing spectres as into his mind there came the tribulations and the insults with which his sullen parishioners had tormented him ever since the ravines had become his last resting place… He saw how old and young had turned their backs on him, hostile and shifty, when he was preaching to them on the holy labour of refurbishing the church which lay in ruins… he saw

how they had all scoffed at the fervour with which on his own
he rebuilt God's house, stone by stone... how, when the church
was repaired, they took that divinely inspired miracle to be
the malign work of the Devil... then he saw how stupefied
they were when, standing before the altar dressed in the sacred
vestments, he made them fall to their knees as he stared them
in the face like a God who had been offended.

But this succession of traumatic visions faded momentarily
when old Mariagna approached his bed dragging with her a
battered lampstand, one of a set that were stored up in the loft
space. The poor woman stood it to the right of the bedhead,
and then went straight away to fetch another, which she placed
opposite. Then she positioned the remaining two by the foot of
the bed, one on each side.

She was extremely patient and meticulous in ensuring that
the lampstands were placed at an equal distance one from
another, carefully checking all the alignments, as if she were
furnishing an altar for a great ceremony. It was as though she
wanted to invest the spectacle of death with all the solemnity
that she could bring to it in her peasant destitution. With the
same display of liturgical ritualism that she had applied to
the methodical placing of the lampstands, she went round to
put each candle in position, lighting them one by one, with a
total air of self-communion and solemn prayer, genuflecting
and crossing herself each time she came close to the bed, just
as if she were performing a hitherto unknown office, one that
she was making up as she went along, dedicated to the eternal
repose of departing souls.

Next she began to arrange the bedside table, to trim the
wick of the lamp, to dust down chairs just like any lady of
the house when they are expecting important visitors to call.
She, poor thing, was that day awaiting a visit from the highest

majesty on earth, a visit from my Lady Death, and she was doing everything she could to welcome her, if not with the correct ceremonial, at least with all the propriety she could bring to the occasion. That is why she was tidying everything, removing fluff and arranging bits of furniture... because what she did not want was to display insufficient reverence or a lack of respect for that mysterious sovereign figure who holds all men in its thrall.

'Death, oh holy Death, when my hour of final agony comes, be kind and gentle with me!' the old woman was muttering, as though praying, while she was arranging the books on the shelf and removing the dust from bundles of papers there, and contemplating what an impressive effect was made by the large candles at each corner of the bed.

XX

Absolution

What a deep shudder was struck in the mind and spirit of the priest by those funereal preparations, as he lay there like a tree trunk, stiff and cold, horrified by his awareness of the burning candle at each corner of his bed! The open grave seemed to be gaping in front of him, ready to receive that body of his in which a soul still flickered... It would not be long before his parishioners arrived to complete their gravediggers' work... not long before the executioners came...

As the memory of the accursed woodlanders was re-awakened in him, he again became feverishly agitated, suddenly affected by a sort of delirium, as though he was writhing once more in the nightmare of the insults and the torments he had been made to suffer. He recalled with horror that Sunday when the Footloose woman came down from Puiggraciós to face up to him inside the very temple, as the sacrament was being performed at the altar... Fortunately he was so steeped in the spirit of the Lord that he had been able to bring her down by dint of conjurations and anathemas, to the

197

terrified wonderment of all the people present. But she had her revenge, the nasty trollop… Because she was the embodiment of the evil spirit of carnality, the scent of womanhood about her had the power to allure the peasants… Thus had she bewitched and entranced them, making them abhor the Mass and the sacraments. And from then on their backs were turned completely on the church as though it were a plague hospice… Old and young, they had all made their way up the slopes to hear the Black Mass at Puiggraciós… Up there a sacrilegious offertory was recited, and they chanted psalms of lechery and derision… But… even so, nothing was as appalling as the night of the Lledonell episode… Such shame and such scandal! To contrive deceitfully for the Body of Christ to be carried over those mountain sides, in order to ambush it and insult it with jeering and mockery… He still seemed to hear that infernal laughter, as he was fleeing with Our Lord's body clutched to his breast… and such wild laughter coming from those diabolical people, *ha, ha! hee, hee!* then his frantic race down the hill, in order to save the consecrated bread and wine from their gibes… running and running without stopping, until he collapsed senseless, not to be picked up until hours later, when they took the Sacrament from him, and then pulled him towards his bed where they laid him, in the place which was now a deathbed, surrounded by candles like a catafalque.

'Oh, what wicked souls! Oh, what fiends! Devils from Hell!' the thoughts in the priest's overagitated mind were spinning around this obsession, when he was suddenly taken by a powerful urge to damn the peasants, to damn them time and again, even though his imprecations would lead to eternal damnation for himself.

It was in the most violently disconcerting part of his nightmare that the priest heard all at once a sad pealing of bells that began to come from the church tower, a sound that announced his death:

Dong... ding... donnng... Ding... dang... dannng!

'Ah, Lord!' he thought in utter terror. 'Ah, Lord, they are ringing my death knell!'

The voice of the bells had never sounded so mournful until that time of supreme anguish. Old Josep, with such feeling of condolence, was making them express their tearful, heart-rending sadness! Each chime was like a desolate sob, like a cry for mercy struggling heavenwards from that vale of tears.

'Have pity, my God, have pity,' prayed the priest in his silent death throes. 'The people from up in the mountains will soon be here, and they will be taking me to the grave before my time and burying me before I have breathed my last...'

Dong... ding... donnng... Ding... dang... dannng... the bells still called out plaintively, as though accompanying with their sobs the silent tragedy, a dying man's tragedy which no one at all would ever know about.

The bitterest part of the priest's last moments, among so many unknown causes of anxiety, was the profound regret at having been unable to dedicate to God's glory all the trials and tribulations he had suffered. Now for the first time, he lamented not having tended each one of them like flowers sprung forth out of pain, in order to offer them up to Christ as penitential posies. But no... all the torments and insults inflicted on him would not stand him in any stead... No... He had never felt, not even in his dreams, that his sufferings were the source of that subtle sweetness which the saints declare they tasted in their own excruciating tribulations... The torments he had undergone in the ravines were too rough, too coarse, for them to provide the soul with the slightest suggestion of sublimity or the faintest hint of delectation… His Calvary had been nothing but the misery of the earth and the blackness of night…

'Pity, Lord,' were the words that kept forming in the consciousness of the dying man, while the bells were being swung with funereal majesty. 'Have pity, Lord, if I have been unable to lift up my eyes to you and if, instead of redeeming the sheep of your flock, I have been dragged down with them into the dirt and the dust…'

Then the bells stopped ringing, and Father Llàtzer thought that the hour of his perdition had come.

'Now the woodlanders will arrive down here,' he thought, 'and they will carry me to the graveyard!'

At that very moment footsteps were heard, apparently of someone coming up the stairs, and the dying man supposed that the brutes from the hillsides were arriving to take him away. His mortal anguish increased as he listened to the sound of the steps coming slowly nearer to the room in which he lay. But in the end it was only old Josep who appeared. Crossing himself as he hobbled past the lighted candles, he went to Mariagna and looking at his wife as if in need of advice, said to her:

'Downstairs there are people from the parish who must have come to see his reverence's corpse…'

Inside his stiffly frozen body, Father Llàtzer's heart gave a start when he heard those words.

'My time is up; this is the end!' he thought. 'Lord, I now commend to you my spirit. Your will be done, now and always!'

'Perhaps we should tell them to come up,' the old woman was saying meanwhile to Josep. 'The sight of death might move their hearts and they might ask forgiveness for the great sins they have committed.'

And as the old man was going back to fetch the parishioners, the priest on his death bed felt some slight relief in his heart, suddenly moved by poor Mariagna's words.

'Maybe that is so,' he thought, 'perhaps the miracle of redemption will now take place. Perhaps, when they think they are looking at my dead body, I shall soften their hearts and make them feel pity, so that they will come to God through the way of compassion.'

But then footsteps were heard again and it was the sound of people coming up to the room. They were the familiar troop, as dull and as glum as ever: crocked old men and heads of households, neighbours from closest to the church, most of them covered in sores like worn-out old hacks ready for the knackers yard.

The first one to show his face was old man Pugna, with his wobbling goitre; then, behind him, Cosme from Rovira, jaundiced and withered; Pere Mestre, with his hopping limp, like a toad; immediately after him, daft Joe Bepus from Uià, ginger-haired and twisted; then Aleix the truffle man, writhing like a snake. Following these near neighbours was another group of parishioners from further away: Pau Malaric, as gaunt as a mummy; old man Sunyer, with his bovine dewlap; Prat from the Black Wood, as hairy as a bear; the old fellow from Lledonell, with a face like an owl's; young master Janet, grim, despondent; young Margaridó, as unapproachable as a wild boar; the youth from Ensulsida, and Carbassot, the swineherd...

It had never been known for the peasants to show reluctance about going to pay respects to a corpse and to say a paternoster over it, and so, as soon as those people heard the death knell being rung, they all felt obliged to make their way down the ravine to where the church stood.

That plaintive sound of the bell, that saddest of all last farewells, was a kind of command that had been obeyed down the generations for countless centuries. Compliance was taken for granted… They just had to bow their heads, resign themselves, and make their way down the mountain side. They had to do as their fathers and grandfathers had done before them, as their remote ancestors had done since time immemorial.

To begin with they had dragged their feet, hesitant, not knowing quite what to do or how to behave. It was such a long time since they had come anywhere near the church that they did not now feel comfortable about making the journey down there. But their indecision lasted only for a moment because they quickly understood that, like it or not, the law of timeless custom and practice, passed down from their forbears, had to be obeyed. Moreover, there was something else, which was that they had immediately begun to feel a strange curiosity about how the priest would look now that he was dead. He had always seemed to them to be so driven and so self-confident, and now they wanted to see how he would look, with his eyes closed, laid out on the catafalque. It was that, that more than anything else, which had finally decided them to leave their houses. And as the parishioners were heading down into the ravine, some of them still hesitant, still rather scared, nervous about going all the way down to the priest's house, Pere Mestre said very sarcastically:

'There's no problem any more… We need not be frightened now about paying him a visit…'

'Too flaming right, 'pon my life! Dead dogs don't bite…' responded Aleix the truffle man with a snigger.

And so they reached the church, quite confident that the priest could no longer confront them like a wrathful God, nor could he use the paten and the chalice to threaten them, nor slander them about their failings and their sins, nor stare at them with that fierce glare of his which pierced their very souls, nor, dressed in his cassock and declaiming from the altar, make them fall to their knees.

As they entered the room where the priest lay dying, the peasants stayed close to the wall looking awkward and embarrassed. Despite being moved by curiosity and the urge to have a good view, they dared not look up, and with their eyes cast down they surveyed askance every part of the room, fixing on the candles and the lampstands, and then, finally, scrutinising the body in the bed.

And, lying there, the poor priest was racked with agonising disquiet to feel how those inquisitive gazes were running all over him, with that sinister curiosity which associations with the grave inspire. Rather than just looking, rather than prying, it was as though they were taking an odd pleasure from sniffing the deathly stench that hung in the air there, around that bed. But finally, as if sickened by the smell, they started to look quite drowsy, quite bemused, seemingly now made anxious as they inwardly absorbed the murky spectacle of death. Old and young gawped dumbly at the scene they beheld.

Although there were so many people gathered in the room, the atmosphere was filled with an unusual stillness and quiet, as though those men were endowed with the mysterious ability to live in complete silence, without ever saying a word or even seeming to breathe, without making any sound whatsoever.

There were those who, as though bewitched, could only stare fixedly at the candles; others, as if under some kind of spell, just stood there open-mouthed and wide-eyed. But the longer that hushed stillness reigned, the more some of them were becoming restless… It was clear that they were not at ease, that they felt strained or nettled, that some kind of deep anxiety was welling up inside them… One of them stuck a finger in his ear… someone else scratched his head… The atmosphere was growing ever tenser as time passed, and the silence seemed eternal… Even for the dying man in his bed of suffering, every instant turned into a century, every hour into an eternity…

'Very soon they will lift me out…' he kept thinking, 'they will wrap me in these sheets… and then take me to the grave…'

But at this moment old Josep appeared among them, carrying a bowl of consecrated water in one hand and the sprinkler in the other.

Despite his bad limp, he now displayed again the measured efficiency he used to have when assisting at Mass in his heyday, a manner which transfigured him into all but a proper priest. Quite unhurriedly, with extreme unction, his spirit possessed by the funeral ceremony he was about to perform, he approached the foot of the bed ready to give the last rites. In order to assist in the prayers, Mariagna moved quickly to kneel by his side, with her arms folded across her chest. They looked just like a real officiating priest and his acolyte who had never in their lives done anything other than perform funeral rites for their dead parishioners.

'Grant him, Lord, eternal peace…' began the old man, as he sprinkled holy water on the catafalque.

And the old woman responded with great fervour:
'And may perpetual light shine upon him.'
'May he rest in peace.'
'Amen.'

The peasants were looking more and more doleful as each

moment passed, more and more deeply pensive, as if they were gradually coming to feel remorse at the sight of death and from the effects of the old couple's devotional zeal. Those flames flickering on the candles, the plaintive tone of the couple's prayers, the sight of the priest, with his pallid lips, with his sunken eyes, his skin ashen and yellowish... everything appeared funereal enough and moving enough to create compassion in the souls of sinners and to bring them to contrition. It was the dreadful vision of the passage from one world to another, with its sequel of eternal glory for those who die in the Lord, or with its accompaniment of eternal suffering and eternal flames for those who die in sin...

Amid the sepulchral silence which reigned in the room a low gasping sound was heard every now and then, as if one of the rustics gathered there had sighed in distress, on the point of bursting into tears...

'...Oh dear... My God! Oh... God!'

Those laments, those sighs reached the ears of the dying priest, and they sounded to him like a delightful choral music. With his infinite faith that his parishioners could be redeemed, he now thought that the hour of their repentance had arrived.

'If only I could speak! If only I could make myself understood,' Father Llàtzer thought, with hope palpitating inside him. 'If I could just take advantage of this moment, the miracle would be sure to happen!'

And suddenly burning with a love of God and of his fellow men, as if in a last surge of the life force, he felt an overwhelming urge to raise his hand and as their priest, to bless them all, saying:

'My brothers, my children, I bless you in the name of the Father, of the Son and of the Holy Spirit!'

Around the bed the woodsmen still stood in a sort of trance, fascinated by the funeral ceremonies which the old couple were performing at intervals. It was as if they were unable to move from where they were, as if they were chained there by some unknown force. There were moments when it seemed that they might be about to show some emotion, to snivel or to burst into tears. It even seemed that, quite unexpectedly, some of them might fall to their knees and join the old couple in reciting the litany...

But then suddenly, just at that critical moment, a bustling noise came from the direction of the door, as though someone was about to come in there unceremoniously and without any effort to respect the silence.

The peasants all turned their heads, taken by surprise and vaguely rubbing their eyes, like people coming out of a deep sleep in which they had been submerged. The first of the new arrivals to show their face was the lass from the Puiggraciós tavern; then came her mother, the innkeeper's wife; and finally, the Footloose woman. All eyes were fixed immediately on the prostitute... and a muttering noise rippled round the room. Footlose looked at the dying man with a repulsive grimace; then she ran her eyes over the rest of the people there, with a look which was both sneering and lascivious... And then she turned tail and left.

A moment of uncertainty affected them all... What to do? What to say? It was pumpkin-face Carbassot who was the first to break rank, followed by Aleix the truffle man, old man Pugna and Cosme from Rovira and daft Bepus from Uià, and then finally, all of the rest of them, all of them, chasing behind the stench exuding from the body of the whore, in a sort of desperation to spread and perpetuate, in those shadowy ravines, those dark vales, the virulence of lust and of suffering.